Rowe

Melanie and the Modeling Mess

The

Twelve Candles Club

Melanie and the Modeling Mess

Elaine L. Schulte

BETHANY HOUSE PUBLISHERS
MINNEAPOLIS, MINNESOTA 55438

Published in association with the literary agency of Alive Communications, P.O. Box 49068, Colorado Springs, CO 80949.

Cover illustration by Andrea Jorgenson

Published by Bethany House Publishers
A Ministry of Bethany Fellowship, Inc.
11300 Hampshire Avenue South
Minneapolis, Minnesota 55438

Printed in the United States of America

Library of Congress Cataloging-in-Publication Data

Schulte, Elaine L.
    Melanie and the modeling mess / Elaine Schulte.
       p. cm. — (The Twelve Candles Club ; bk. 5)
    Summary: Uneasy about her Chinese heritage but determined to fit into her new southern California neighborhood, Melanie Lin's offer to find modeling jobs for the girls in the Twelve Candles Club leads to trouble.
    [1. Moving, Household—fiction. 2. Friendship—Fiction. 3. Clubs—Fiction. 4. Chinese-Americans—Fiction. 5. California—Fiction. 6. Christian life—Fiction.] I. Title. II. Series: Schulte, Elaine L. Twelve Candles Club ; 5.
PZ7.S3867Me   1994
[Fic]—dc20   93-45377
                                            CIP

ISBN 1-55661-254-0   AC

ELAINE L. SCHULTE is the well-known author of twenty-five novels for women and children. Over one million copies of her popular books have been sold. She received a Distinguished Alumna Award from Purdue University as well as numerous other awards for her work as an author. After living in various places, including several years in Europe, she and her husband make their home in San Diego, California, where she writes full time.

CHAPTER

1

Kneeling on her bedroom window seat, Melanie Lin peered down the louvers of her shutters. Beyond the cul-de-sac, across the street, she saw the Twelve Candles Club girls marching sideways . . . CLOMP, CLOMP, CLOMP . . . on the sidewalk.

"Order in the court . . . the monkey wants to speak . . . speak, monkey, speak!" the four girls chorused. "Order in the court, the monkey wants to speak. . . !"

They might be crazy in the head, like Auntie Ying-Ying said, but they looked very interesting. Besides, Melanie had already seen one of their wild escapades on TV, and it was definitely fun.

They still marched sideways, and Melanie almost laughed aloud. *Now's the time to go out to meet them*, she told herself. No more excuses about why they wouldn't be friends. She'd pretend she was going to look at the neighborhood garage sale items set out on tables across the street.

She grabbed her wallet from the clutter on top of her white desk. *Maybe I'd better buy something.*

As she headed for her bedroom door, she glimpsed herself in the full-length mirror that hung behind it: a cloud of flowing black hair, brown almond-shaped eyes, a thin body under white shorts and a white Tee, and white leather thongs on her narrow feet.

She stopped at the mirror, pushing her slanted eyes in at the sides to make them rounder, then opening them wide to show more white. If her eyes would just stay like that, she wouldn't look quite so Chinese—not that all Chinese had such slanted eyes.

Her skinny ten-year-old brother, William, stepped into the upstairs hallway, his brown eyes shining with mischief. He pretended to be a kung fu expert, and stood waiting for her. Making a quick hand chop toward her, he shouted a fierce, "Hiii-ee-yah!"

Melanie dodged him. "Stop it, William!" She wished he'd never heard of kung fu, even if it was the most honorable of ancient Chinese fighting arts.

"Where you going?" he asked as she rushed on.

"Just outside. You are *not* invited." He was so crazy about kung fu lately it was embarrassing. Worse, even old Auntie Ying-Ying had picked up his wild kung fu yell.

"You going out riding with Fender-Bender?" he asked. He ran his fingers through his thick black hair as if he wanted to go out riding, too.

"Connie's already out practicing her driving," Melanie answered. That alone explained why they'd begun to call their twenty-year-old cousin Fender-Bender. She hadn't needed to drive when they lived in New York.

He looked disappointed for a moment. Chopping the air again, he let out another loud "Hiii-ee-yah!"

"Stop it!"

Dad called her brother Kung Fu Willie, but he also called *her* Jabberwacky Melanie because she talk-talk-talked when she got nervous. Well, she would definitely not jabber when she met the girls.

As she hurried out her front door, the Twelve Candles Club girls stood in a driveway, chorusing another "Order in the court. . . !"

Melanie made herself stroll calmly down her front walk, then across the small cul-de-sac to La Crescenta, their main street. Now some of the little kids, probably sisters and brothers, marched along sideways with the four girls, laughing and yelling with them.

The reddish blond girl picked up a wooden spoon from a table and repeated into it, "Speak, monkey, speak!"

Women and older kids sold things from the nearby tables, and one of them called out, "You crazy kids!"

Melanie put a hand to her lips to keep from laughing. What she wouldn't give to have some fun—and to have some good friends here.

The reddish blond girl noticed her first. She gave a friendly smile and asked, "Aren't you the new girl? . . . the one who moved into a house on the cul-de-sac?"

Melanie nodded. "Right. I'm Melanie Lin. We moved in a month ago, but we've been . . . we've been busy getting settled." It'd be best to impress them right off, she decided, and paused for effect. "And I had some . . . jobs to get going."

"Jobs?" asked the short, athletic-looking girl. She wore a

9

white Tee that spelled out JESS in green letters.

Melanie nodded again.

"We work too," the JESS T-shirt girl said. "What do you do?"

Melanie put on her most calm and collected expression. "Modeling. I do modeling."

"MODELING?!" all four exclaimed, even more impressed than she'd hoped.

"I used to work in New York City," she added, "so I had to interview to find just the right southern California agent." She was not about to tell them that her new agent—Ms. Schivitz—was not "just the right one." In fact, she was downright rude, and Mom suspected she was slightly unscrupulous—that she'd have to watch her carefully. Worse, Ms. Schivitz was the only agent who'd accept her, because the other agencies already had plenty of Asian models.

The girls stood there so speechless about the modeling that Melanie rushed on. "And you know how much work there is to moving, too."

"Becky and I have lived in the same houses since we were born, so we've never moved," the reddish blond said. "By the way, I'm Tricia Bennett." She gestured to the tall, slim girl with dark hair. "This is Becky Hamilton." And to the quiet girl, "This is Cara Hernandez . . . and, wearing the JESS Tee, is Jess McColl."

"Hi," Melanie said. "I heard about your Twelve Candles Club on TV the week we moved in."

Becky rolled her blue eyes. "Didn't everyone?!"

Melanie smiled. "I read about the robber you caught, too."

"Don't even mention that!" Jess McColl replied so fiercely that they all laughed.

Melanie tried to remember their names. Tricia Bennett—the outgoing reddish blond with green eyes . . . Becky Hamilton—tall, brown hair and blue eyes . . . Cara Hernandez—shy and Hispanic, black hair, brown eyes . . . Jess McColl—short and athletic, brown hair and hazel eyes.

Jess asked, "How old are you, anyhow?"

"I . . . ah . . . almost twelve," Melanie answered, knowing she was younger than the four girls. "In fact, tomorrow's my birthday."

"We're all twelve, too," Becky put in. "And the only twelve-year-olds on the entire street."

All the more important to make friends with them, Melanie told herself. So far, there was no sign of any other ABCs—American-Born Chinese—around.

"Did you live right in New York City?" Cara asked.

"No . . . in a nearby suburb. But there was public transportation, which was great for getting into the city without a car, and just about anywhere else," Melanie answered. She raised her brows, then let out a disappointed breath. "We're still not used to having to drive everywhere."

Melanie hoped it didn't sound like complaining, but the lack of public transportation was the one thing her family didn't like about southern California life.

"We get around a lot on our bikes," Jess said. "We can ride clear down to the ocean, and all around for shopping . . . and best of all, to our jobs."

Just then, a car drove down their street, and Melanie stepped up onto a small strip of lawn between the street and sidewalk.

"You know," Tricia said, "you may be able to help us out! We have . . . well, you heard about our Twelve Candles Club.

Our latest problem is that we're getting too busy. Do you baby-sit?"

Melanie hesitated. "Not much. I have a younger sister and brother, but my aunt and grandmother have always lived nearby, so they've done the baby-sitting."

"Too bad," Becky said. "Besides, with your looks, you're probably too busy modeling."

Melanie blushed at the compliment.

"I'm not very busy modeling here yet," she admitted. The fact was that she didn't know when she'd get modeling jobs in Santa Rosita—if ever. Worst of all, most of her modeling money was in savings for college. The rest she'd spent on presents for her ABC friends in New York just before she'd left.

After a moment, Jess asked, "Did you come to the neighborhood garage sale to buy something?"

The blunt question took Melanie by surprise, and she began to look at the items on the driveway tables: toys, lamps, games, linens, fabrics, used clothes, and kitchen stuff. Old bikes, skateboards, and three-wheelers stood on the lawns and the driveways. "Depends on what I find, I guess."

"Here's a pretty perfume bottle for sale," Becky suggested, holding it up for her to inspect.

Melanie shook her head. "I'm allergic to perfume."

One of the mothers had just finished selling used draperies, and she turned to Melanie. "I'm Becky's mother. Was it your father who sang at the Santa Rosita Community Church last Sunday?"

Melanie nodded. "Yes, it was."

Mrs. Hamilton beamed. "He sings wonderfully. I really enjoyed it."

"Thanks—"

Tricia interrupted, "You mean you go there?"

"My parents visited different churches before the rest of us moved here, and they really liked it at the Community Church," Melanie explained. It occurred to her that her father was probably the first Chinese-American who'd ever been asked to sing in their church; that's why Becky's mother had noticed. Maybe they didn't even know that lots of Chinese were Christians.

"Whoa, great!" Tricia said. "Becky and I go there, too. And Jess and Cara have just started coming this summer."

Melanie felt a wave of hope, though they hadn't actually invited her to go with them. She decided not to ask, either. Luckily, another car passed by on the street, and the driver waved at Tricia and Becky.

After a moment, Jess said, "We've all been wondering why you put up the big wall in front of the houses. Not that it isn't interesting."

Probably they thought that Chinese people were weird, Melanie worried as she turned around and eyed the white stucco wall. Three gray sea gulls in flight filled the right upper side, and a brass strip like a sunset curved over the lower section. A real willow tree stood just to the left of the wall, and a carpet of purple ice plant bloomed all the way out to the street. Behind the wall, you could see the second stories of the two white houses and their red-tiled roofs, and, between them, the red-tiled roof of the covered courtyard.

"My mom's an artist," Melanie explained. "She came with my dad months ago, before the rest of us, to get the houses remodeled and the landscaping and the wall and everything else done."

"Why did you buy two houses?" Cara asked.

"My uncle's family and mine want to live close together, but . . . you know . . . we each have our own house."

"It looks very attractive," Mrs. Hamilton remarked. "In fact, it's rather nice to have more variety in Santa Rosita Estates. Most of our houses look somewhat alike."

Whew! Melanie thought with relief. They didn't think the wall looked as if it belonged in front of a Chinese restaurant like Uncle Gwo-Jenn said. And it was true that all of the houses had red tile roofs, though some were one story and some were two, and they were painted different colors.

Her relief stopped a moment later, though.

Coming around "The Great Wall of China" were Auntie Ying-Ying and Grandmother Lin. Both were dressed as if they were "FOB Chinese"—fresh-off-the-boat. Gray-haired Auntie Ying-Ying wore a red Chinese blouse and black pants, and white-haired Grandmother Lin wore all black. They were both big bargain hunters and hurried along as if all of the good deals might escape.

Worse, the four girls were staring at them.

For an instant, Melanie's white thongs felt rooted to the lawn under her feet. *Do something fast*, she told herself.

She spoke very quickly. "You know, you're all so different and interesting looking, I think I might be able to get you modeling jobs."

"You're kidding!" Jess exclaimed, turning to her.

Unsure as she felt about it, Melanie shook her head. "I'm not kidding."

"I can see why they'd want you to model. But us. . . ?" Jess asked. "You really think they'd take klutzes like us?"

Melanie swallowed, then plunged ahead. "One of the advertising agencies is looking for all kinds of kids. At least that's what I heard in an agent's office."

Probably she shouldn't have mentioned it until she knew more details. But it was the only way she could imagine getting these girls to be her friends, with Auntie Ying-Ying and Grandmother Lin on the way here. "I'd have to talk to my agent, though."

"How soon would we know?" Becky asked.

"I'll talk to her Monday," Melanie answered. She only hoped Ms. Schivitz wouldn't be furious if she phoned her. The agent's last words had been, "Don't call me, I'll call you."

"What would we have to do?" Cara asked. "I've never done modeling."

"Just model back-to-school clothes, maybe for newspaper ads . . . probably in a group setting."

They seemed so stunned by the idea that she jabbered on. "Look, you don't have to worry. I'd teach you everything you'd need to know. My cousin Connie can take pictures of you to submit to my agent. Connie's very good at photography."

"Glad to hear it," Tricia said. "Anyhow, it'd sure be interesting. And it probably pays a lot more than baby-sitting."

"It pays pretty well, especially in New York City or Los Angeles. It's not nearly as good here, though."

"I've never met a model before," Jess said.

Melanie smiled. "There are over ten thousand kid models in the country, but I'd guess there's not too many here."

"Ten thousand?" Becky echoed.

Melanie nodded. "That includes everything from print to broadcast." They looked a little confused, so she added, "You know, print means newspapers, catalogs, magazines, brochures, billboards . . . and even boxes and packages."

"Boxes and packages?" Jess repeated.

"Sure. Food boxes, playpen packages . . . even the babies on some diaper boxes."

"I hadn't thought about all of that," Jess answered. "What have you done?"

"Mostly fashion prints for magazines and catalogs, but a few TV commercials, like for Coca-Cola and IBM."

"Whoa!" Tricia exclaimed. "I'm impressed!"

A good thing, too, Melanie decided. From the corner of her eye, she saw Grandmother and Auntie Ying-Ying examining a pile of fabric at the next table and slowly working their way toward her. Auntie had probably heard every word about the modeling jobs. It wasn't long before she had edged to their table.

"You think you buy skateboard?" Auntie teased Melanie, glancing just below the curb and grinning.

Melanie saw a battered skateboard that must have rolled down from the lawn and now stood near the curb at the edge of the street. Before she could say, "No way!" Auntie added, "Good California transportation, hah? Maybe you good at it. Like when you go ice-skating at Rockefeller Center?"

When Auntie Ying-Ying spoke, it was best to answer, so Melanie said agreeably, "Good transportation, all right." She just hoped Auntie Ying-Ying wouldn't make a spectacle of herself, letting loose with one of William's wild "Hiii-ee-yahs."

Grandmother Lin only smiled sweetly, which was lucky. She spoke mostly Chinese, and Auntie Ying-Ying usually talked enough for both of them.

Now Auntie asked, "You not introduce us to new friends?"

"Sure, Auntie." She turned to the girls, who were staring at her aunt and grandmother. "I would like to introduce my aunt and grandmother, both named Mrs. Lin. . . ."

Auntie beamed and bobbed her head. "Okay you call me Auntie Ying-Ying. What you girls' names?"

Melanie rushed on, "This is Becky . . . and Cara . . . and Tricia . . . and Jess—"

"You not know *you own* names?" Auntie Ying-Ying joked.

It took a moment for them to get her joke, then they all grinned back, saying "Hi" or "It's nice to meet you."

Melanie hoped Auntie and Grandmother Lin would move on, but once Auntie started talking, she was hard to stop.

"You come visit Melanie," she told the girls. "Melanie has good room. New paint . . . new furniture, bedspreads. . . . Very nice!"

Before the girls could reply, Auntie Ying-Ying's mouth opened wide at a thought. "You come tomorrow! We already plan fine birthday party for her. Good Chinese food! You come five o'clock! Yes, you come!"

The girls looked uneasily at Melanie, who felt uneasy herself. Even the promise of modeling jobs for them might not be enough to overcome the shock of one of Auntie Ying-Ying's dinners.

"Sure," Melanie said, not having much choice. "You're all four invited. We're going to use the new table outside in the courtyard." She gave a little laugh. "It's behind 'The Great Wall of China,' as my father calls it."

She waited for them to say they were busy, that they had other plans, but Jess said, "Hey, it sounds different." Then she asked the others, "How about it?"

"Let me ask my mom," Becky said, bobbing her head a little at Auntie Ying-Ying, then hurrying off.

"Me too," Tricia added. "Be back in a minute."

All four of them took off, and Melanie realized they were

all interested in coming, which was a hopeful sign.

"See?" Auntie Ying-Ying declared. "Good party . . . maybe they bring good birthday presents."

"Please, Auntie . . . please let me make friends myself . . . in my own way."

"You way too slow," Auntie said. "Best to make move right away. You ask Auntie. Get good advice."

Her aunt always meant well, Melanie knew. If only she didn't make such a spectacle of herself. Melanie kept her lips shut, bowing a little and backing away slowly to the street. *I'll just edge away politely*, she thought, stepping down.

Suddenly one foot landed on the middle of the battered skateboard with such force that it rolled out away from the curb, with her on it. "Yiiiiiii!" Melanie squealed, trying to catch her balance as she continued rolling backwards. She flung her arms back, but the skateboard only jerked and changed direction, going downhill.

A car honked, and Melanie looked up long enough to see wide-eyed Cousin Connie behind the wheel. She screeched it to a halt, while Melanie skidded backwards, teetering precariously on the skateboard.

"Melanieeeeeeee, what you doing on street?!" Auntie Ying-Ying shrieked for the whole neighborhood to hear, clutching her chest with both hands. "What you doing. . . ? W-h-a-t y-o-u d-o-i-n-g. . . ?" Pointing at Melanie, she let loose an even louder yell that turned both of them into spectacles. "Hiii-ee-yah!"

Just then the skateboard hit a rut, and Melanie landed on the asphalt with a thud. She heard people gasp, but once they saw she was not seriously hurt, their concern turned into laughter. And Melanie wished with all of her heart that she could disappear.

CHAPTER

2

The next morning as she dressed for church, Melanie's mind darted back to the awful moment the skateboard hit the bump and sent her flying onto the road. She'd scraped the rough asphalt with her right knee and right hand.

Jess, Cara, Becky, and Tricia had all come running. "You all right?" they'd asked, as if they really cared. Embarrassed and shaky, she'd picked herself up and tried to brush off the dirt and bits of gravel. Her hand didn't hurt too much, but her knee looked bad. She wouldn't cry . . . she just wouldn't . . . no matter how much it hurt.

"Melanie Lin!" Auntie Ying-Ying had called out. "You give poor old auntie heart attack!"

The girls had glanced at Auntie Ying-Ying, then looked back at her almost as if they couldn't quite make up their minds about the new Chinese neighbors. Well, with Auntie Ying-Ying around, she couldn't blame them.

Melanie chose a white sundress from her closet. She'd have to wear white tights to cover the scab forming on her right knee. And she'd have to phone Ms. Schivitz tomorrow and tell her no modeling—at least, none that involved knees—until her knee was back to normal. What an embarrassing episode— just as she was getting to know the neighborhood girls . . . and just as she was beginning her southern California modeling career.

She pulled the white sundress over her head and smoothed it down. The dress looked nice with her white tights, and she decided on a purple sash around the waist to give the dress more interest and color.

Her outfit was a lot like her modern-style bedroom: white walls, white carpet, white comforters on the twin beds. Pure white looked great with bold dashes of the primary colors she'd chosen—emerald green, royal purple, and cherry red—which covered the four floor pillows around the window seat, the piles of throw pillows on it, and the beds' throw pillows. Her modeling job pictures on the walls, especially the colorful skiing and beach shots, also added interest.

A knock sounded at the door, and Mom said, "It's me, birthday girl. Do you need help dressing?"

"Maybe," Melanie answered. "My hand still hurts."

Mom let herself in, smiling. "Happy birthday, skateboarder," she teased, her dark eyes dancing.

"Thanks a lot!"

Mom gave a little laugh. "If only Connie had taken a picture of your ride down the street."

"Especially the fall. It was soooooo embarrassing."

Mom dropped a kiss on Melanie's forehead. "You know I'm only teasing. Here, let me help with your sash."

"And my sandals," Melanie added. "My hand and knee still feel stiff. It was hard to get on my tights. And I didn't do a good job brushing my hair."

Her mother tied the purple sash around Melanie's waist. "There," she said, standing back and fussing until it was perfect. "Now sit down on your bed. It's been a long time since I've put on your shoes. Let's see if I remember how." She smiled as she sat down on Melanie's bed with her. "Hmmm, I believe your feet are bigger. It's hard to believe I am the mother of a twelve-year-old."

Melanie grinned as she sat back against the colorful throw pillows. Usually she hated help, but today it was nice for Mom to take over again. Besides, she liked to look at her.

As usual, Mom was simply dressed, highlighting her dark beauty. This morning she wore a green linen dress, and her long black hair was done up in a twist poked through with ivory chopsticks. Her slanted dark eyes added mysteriousness. Even her hands and slim fingers had an elegance about them, though she wore no nail polish and only a gold wedding band. She looked just like someone named Jade Lin should and, best of all, she scarcely had any accent since she'd come to the U.S. when she was only four years old.

Mom finished buckling the first white sandal. "Do you want to sit with us in church again or go to the youth group with your new friends?"

"Maybe I'll go to the youth group," Melanie decided. She hadn't stopped feeling stupid about her wild skateboard ride, but according to Auntie Ying-Ying, the girls were still coming this afternoon for her birthday dinner. She'd better be with them this morning, so they'd know it wasn't just Auntie's idea.

Down the hall, brother William gave out a wild "Hiii-ee-yah!" and five-year-old Silvee shouted "Quit it!" back at him.

"I wish he'd stop doing that stupid kung fu yell," Melanie said. "Even Auntie Ying-Ying is using it."

"It's just a phase," Mom replied. Smiling, she shook her head herself. "Let's hope they'll both get over it."

"Let's hope so!"

Mom finished buckling Melanie's other shoe, then stood up and went to the white dressing table for the hair brush. She brushed Melanie's hair on top first, then Melanie bent over, and her mother brushed it from underneath to give it fullness. "Okay, up."

It was an old hair routine for Melanie, who straightened up and shook her head a little so her hair could settle. Mom gave it a few more swipes with the brush to shape it. "There, you look just perfect. Ready?"

Melanie stiff-legged her way to the back-of-the-door mirror. "My hair does look good and full."

Her mother mimicked a fashion show commentator. "And here we have Melanie Lin wearing a lovely white sundress, white tights, and white sandals, and a perfect cloud of black hair."

Melanie rolled her eyes.

"Let's go, birthday girl."

Melanie stiff-legged along the hallway behind her mother and was glad to see that William was already heading down the stairs. No kung fu chop this morning, *if* she were lucky.

Downstairs in the breakfast area, Dad put aside the Sunday newspaper and stood up. Smiling, he started singing in his nice deep baritone voice, "Happy birthday to you . . ." He looked so handsome with his strong chin, long narrow nose, and beautiful white smile. And the love in his brown eyes filled her heart with joy.

Beside him, Silvee beamed at her sweetly, her dark eyes shining as she stood and sang. She wore her royal blue dress with tiny red flowers, white anklets, and cute little red shoes. A matching royal blue headband separated her bangs and long dark hair, making her look even more darling.

When they sang "dear Melanie," she knew that her family meant it . . . at least Mom and Dad and Silvee. Lately, she wasn't so sure about William, who grinned at her mischievously as they hit the final "Happy birthday to you!" At least he didn't end it with a "Hiii-ee-yah!"

Dad came around the table to give her a hug and a kiss, then came Mom and Silvee, and even William, who made his kiss loud and sloppy.

"Uffff!" Melanie complained.

"I can see you're going to charm the young ladies someday with that kind of kissing," Dad teased him.

William blushed, then laughed a phoney "Ha-ha, ho-ho!" as if he would never stoop that low.

"Whatever you do, don't encourage him in that direction, Charlie!" Mom warned.

Dad grinned at her. His first name was really Chung, but she'd always called him Charlie, and the other doctors at the New York hospital where he'd worked had called him Charlie too. Probably he'd told the ones at Santa Rosita General to do the same. And the church bulletin last Sunday had announced a solo by Dr. Charles Lin. He'd told them Charlie, but someone must have decided that Charles sounded better for a church bulletin. He didn't have much of a Chinese accent, either, because he'd come to the U.S. when he was twelve.

Dad sat down at the round white table again. "Silvee and I have already said grace," he said, meaning they'd have to pray by themselves.

Melanie sat down in her white chair between Mom and Silvee. Their blue and white stoneware Chinese dishes lay on new roughly woven white place mats, and the orange juice had been poured into the small glasses. It was a nice table and nice dishes and nice food in a very nice house, Melanie told herself. She had lots for which to be grateful.

Bowing her head, she tried to think what to pray. She'd been going to church all of her life, but she'd never been good at making up prayers. Finally, she prayed the usual "God is great and God is good. Let us thank Him for our food. Amen." The words seemed empty today, though, which made her feel bad.

Looking up, she saw Dad give her a pleased smile. She quickly reached for a bran muffin and blueberry jam. Maybe now that she was twelve, she should learn more about praying . . . and about God.

Later, they piled into the backseat of Dad's white Buick. As usual, Melanie sat on the right side, and Silvee sat between her and William to keep things more peaceful. Driving down La Crescenta, they passed Becky's and Tricia's houses in time to see both girls piling into the Bennetts' minivan.

"It looks as if your new friends attend church," Dad remarked as they drove along.

He and Mom nodded at Mrs. Bennett from the front seat, and Mrs. Bennett nodded and smiled back.

"They go to Santa Rosita Community Church, too," Melanie told him. "Becky's mother told me she enjoyed your singing last Sunday."

Mom smiled at Dad. "Becky's mother has very fine taste."
He gave a hearty laugh.

Silvee had been leaning forward to peer past Melanie out the side window. "What're your friends' names?"

"Those two are Becky Hamilton and Tricia Bennett. The two others coming to my party are Jess McColl and Cara Hernandez."

William grinned. "Just wait till they come over," he warned. "Just wait!"

"Don't you dare be stupid around them!" Melanie told him. "You're not going to ruin my birthday!"

Silvee shook a chubby finger at him. "You be good, William. You be good for Melanie's birthday party."

He grinned right past her at Melanie. "Just wait," he warned again. "You just wait!"

"Dad. . . !" Melanie began, then saw that he and Mom were in a serious discussion. Well, she'd tell them later. For now, she raised her chin and gave William a look of pure disgust.

Glancing back, she saw Uncle Gwo-Jenn and Auntie Ying-Ying's red Buick behind them, with Grandmother and Grandfather Lin sitting in the backseat. If only she could have a real birthday party, one *without* her family! But that wasn't the Chinese way. At least not the way of this Chinese family.

The white stucco buildings of Santa Rosita Community Church were topped by red tile roofs and surrounded by lots of trees. Red geraniums bloomed around the bright green lawn, making it look cheerful and welcoming. Already, cars filled the parking lot, and people streamed toward the buildings.

Mom and Dad had stopped their discussion, so Melanie asked her father out of courtesy, "Do you suppose I could go to youth group this morning?"

"Good idea," Dad replied as he drove the Buick into a parking space. "Maybe this morning's a good time for all of you to try Sunday school."

"All of us?!" William objected.

"That's what I said," their father answered firmly.

Your fault! William mouthed at Melanie. *I'll get you!*

She raised her chin again and turned away. Looking out the window, she noticed Tricia's mother was parking their maroon minivan just four spaces down from them. They must have driven fast or taken a shortcut because Jess and Cara were in the van, too.

"There's the neighbor girls," she said. She hadn't planned to walk in with them, but anything was better than being dragged along with William. Besides, Uncle Gwo-Jenn and Auntie Ying-Ying were parking their car right next to them.

Melanie spoke quickly. "I'll go with the girls to the youth group room."

"Good idea," Mom replied. "We'll meet you out front when the service is over."

The moment Dad turned off the engine, Melanie jumped out, almost forgetting about her stiff knee. "See you!" she told them. She only hoped that the Twelve Candles Club girls wouldn't mind taking her . . . or being in the company of a stiff-kneed Chinese girl.

She smoothed her hair and headed for the minivan.

"Whoa! It's Melanie!" Tricia exclaimed as she climbed out of the van's sliding door.

Becky was right behind her. "Hey, all right!"

Melanie felt sure her family was watching, and she hoped

one of the girls would think to invite her along, but they were too busy getting out of the minivan. "Mind if I go along to the youth group room with you?" she asked.

"Mind?" Tricia repeated. "No way! Come on!"

Melanie hoped she wasn't just saying it to be polite. She turned back and, sure enough, her family was watching.

Worse, Auntie Ying-Ying was shouting, "Happy birthday, Melanieee! Happy birthday!"

Uncle Gwo-Jenn and Grandmother and Grandfather Lin called out more "Happy birthdays!" to her, too.

Melanie cringed. "Thanks. See you all later!"

Cara and Jess had climbed out of van and were looking from her family to her.

"I-I just thought I'd rather go to the youth group room with you guys than have my parents dragging me along," Melanie told them. "It's not easy, being new."

Cara's brown eyes filled with sympathy. "I know what you mean. Jess and I are still new at church, too. Not that such a minor matter would bother Jess."

Jess grinned. "Guess you could say I'm not exactly shy."

"Now that's an understatement," Tricia put in, and they all laughed a little.

Tricia's mother smiled at Melanie as she corralled her two younger kids. "Happy birthday! The girls are all looking forward to your party this afternoon. It was nice of your aunt to invite them."

"Thanks," Melanie responded, wondering what they really thought of Auntie Ying-Ying.

"Yeah, happy birthday!" the girls called out, making people all around them look.

"Thanks," Melanie said again.

"Come on," Tricia told them, and they all trooped through the cars in the parking lot.

Melanie tried not to walk stiffly, but it wasn't easy with a sore knee. As they made their way toward the church buildings, her leg may as well have been a big bamboo stalk.

"You all right?" Jess asked as they reached the sidewalk.

Melanie nodded. "Not perfect, but all right."

"I get lots of injuries from gymnastics," Jess said. "I know what it feels like."

"I had to wear tights to cover my knee," Melanie admitted.

Becky must have overheard, because she looked at Melanie's tights, then remarked, "Hey, don't we all look nice? Like flowers, my sister always says."

She was wearing a blue sundress with a tiny white butterfly pattern; Tricia wore a light green dress with white swirls; Cara, a striped pink-and-white with puff sleeves; and Jess, a plain peach-colored sundress.

Melanie decided that her white sundress fit in, even if her white tights did seem a bit much. As a model, maybe she should stand out a little, but, at the moment, it felt lots more comfortable to fit in. Now, if she just didn't take up jabbering to hide her nervousness.

When they arrived in the classroom, twenty or more kids were already sitting around in the tan folding chairs. Most of them were talking, but they sneaked glances at her.

"Hi, everybody," Tricia said to them. "We've brought a new neighbor, Melanie Lin. She's not only a New York model, but a skateboarding champion."

Melanie couldn't help giving a laugh. "Not a skateboarding champion!"

Everyone in the room looked interested now, and Tricia

began to introduce them. "And this is Bear, our youth minister," she said. "His real name is Ted. You know, Ted, as in Teddy Bear."

"Hi," Melanie said.

"Glad to have you here, Melanie," he answered, looking as if he meant it. "But I was hoping you were a skateboarding champion."

She laughed again, feeling better. "Don't even mention it!"

"If you say so, I won't," he told her, his blue eyes full of good humor, "though it sounds as if there's a good story behind it."

She shook her head, still grinning.

"Welcome," he added, then moved toward the front of the bright sunlit room.

He wasn't at all like the tall and rather formal youth minister in New York. Instead, he was short, broad-shouldered, and did sort of look like a cozy Teddy Bear, Melanie decided. He wore baggy cotton pants and a wild flowered shirt. What's more, he'd brought along a guitar, which he began to strap around his neck now.

"Good morning, gang," he said, then strummed a chord on his guitar to quiet everyone.

"Good morning, Bear!" the kids echoed, as if they did the same greeting every Sunday morning.

After Melanie and another new girl were introduced, Bear made sure everyone had song sheets. Then he began the singing with "He's Got the Whole World in His Hands," which Melanie knew from New York, then moved on to "Leaning on the Everlasting Arms."

Melanie peered around over her song sheet. There was something different about these youth group kids. Most of them seemed to really mean the words they were singing, especially when they sang the next song, "Bless the Lord." On either side of her, Tricia and Becky closed their eyes as they sang, and a special sweetness seemed to surround them.

"What an awesome God we serve," Bear said, taking off his guitar. "What an awesome God."

Melanie didn't quite understand what Bear meant about serving Him. For one thing, God seemed faraway to her.

Bear made announcements, then asked, "Anyone else have big news?"

Tricia waved her hand. "Today is Melanie's twelfth birthday."

"Hey-hey!" Bear returned, grinning at her. "Happy birthday! That makes it even more special that you're here. How about you standing up with Melanie, Tricia, while we give her our usual rousing birthday greeting?"

Melanie was glad to have Tricia standing with her as everyone sang "Happy Birthday" as loud as they could. On the final line, they pointed at her, grinning, and howled, "Happy birthday to you!"

"Thanks," Melanie said, sitting down fast.

Luckily one of the boys had celebrated his birthday last week, and they all sang him a rowdy chorus, too.

Finally the announcements were done, and Bear said, "We've discussed the Ten Commandments the last two Sundays. I thought we might start today with other questions. Anyone have a question?"

No one raised a hand, and Melanie felt more and more nervous as he looked at her. Suddenly she jabbered, "Can you tell us what Jewish people believe? I have a Jewish friend in New York. . . ."

Everyone seemed to be staring at her, and she smoothed the skirt of her white sundress with clammy hands, wishing she'd kept her mouth shut. Why did she always have to jabber when she felt nervous?

"Good question," Bear replied. "I'll repeat it. What do Jewish people believe? Basically, they believe that the Messiah is still coming. Christians believe that He's Jesus Christ and that He was here once and is coming back again. Also, that He lives in our hearts now. Unfortunately, some Christians don't live as if they know Jesus."

He smiled at Melanie. "Does that answer your question?"

She nodded, although it wasn't entirely clear to her. What did he mean by "knowing Jesus". . . ?

And what did he mean by "Some Christians don't live as if they know Jesus"?

It struck her that maybe she was one of them!

CHAPTER

3

Just before five o'clock, Melanie wandered outside to the covered courtyard between the two houses. This family birthday party could ruin her growing friendship with the Twelve Candles Club girls, she reminded herself nervously. If only she and her family weren't so different from everyone else in the neighborhood. *Why* did they have to be so Chinese? Why . . . why . . . why. . . ?

She pushed back her hair and straightened her aqua shorts and top outfit. Upstairs in her mirror, she'd looked nice, except for the big bandage over her knee. She just hoped that the girls would dress casual, too.

Melanie sat hidden by "The Great Wall of China," but she could already hear Jess, Cara, Becky, and Tricia talking as they crossed the street to the cul-de-sac. Maybe they were only coming because they were curious about her and her family.

"Hey, Melanieeeeee," Auntie Ying-Ying called out. She

wore her red silk Chinese dress and hurried from her house to the covered courtyard, carrying a punch bowl full of pink lemonade. "You friends come now, chop-chop! I told you it be a good party!"

"Thanks, Auntie Ying-Ying," Melanie said, trying to sound grateful. Her auntie, who prided herself on her cooking, had done much of the work for dinner and she did mean well. "What do you want me to do?"

"No work," her aunt answered. "Have good time on birthday. Connie and rest of family helps."

Melanie saw the girls approaching her front door, luckily wearing shorts outfits similar to hers. They carried birthday presents, too. "Over here!" she yelled, hurrying to them. "We're having the party in the courtyard."

"Whoa . . . isn't this nice?" Tricia said as the four of them headed for the courtyard.

"All right!" Jess agreed.

Cara and Becky looked impressed, too.

Probably they'd never seen a covered courtyard like this: thick bamboo stalks tied under the peaked roof . . . red ceramic Chinese lanterns hanging over the long red-tiled table and benches . . . extra seating benches at the outer edges of the courtyard . . . a huge wok by the built-in barbecue. At least it was private—the two white houses on either side, the wall in front, and in the back, a hillside covered with purple ice plant.

"See!" Auntie Ying-Ying called out to Melanie. "They like! They like! They bring birthday presents too!"

Melanie felt her face turning red.

Tricia grinned. "Where should we put the presents?"

Melanie looked around. "Over on the end of the table by

the punch bowl, I guess. May as well have some punch while we're at it, too."

"I get punch cups, chop-chop!" Auntie Ying-Ying exclaimed, running for her house again.

"What's *chop-chop*?" Cara asked.

"Fast," Melanie answered, her face still warm. "You know, like 'in a hurry.' It's sort of a family joke."

Moments later, her parents and Silvee and William came from the kitchen door, carrying baskets with dishes and silverware. Mom looked nice in her crinkly white blouse and slacks . . . Dad, handsome in a white shirt and tan bermudas . . . Silvee, cute in her pink sundress . . . and William, skinnier and more peculiar than ever in his black pants, red shirt, and red-and-white striped sweater, as if it were freezing outside.

William pretended not to notice her guests, and he cut the air with a wild kung fu chop and yelled a fierce "Hiii-ee-yah!"

"Brothers. . . !" Melanie complained, wondering where his brain was hidden.

"You know it," Jess agreed. "I've got three myself, only mine are all older."

"They couldn't be weirder than William," Melanie said.

"You want to bet?" Jess asked. "For beginners, Jordan puts mayonnaise on tacos and spaghetti . . . and just about everything else—"

"William puts soy sauce on spaghetti . . . even on ice cream!" Melanie said. "Besides that and his crazy kung fu chops, he tells stupid jokes."

"How old is he?" Tricia asked.

"Ten. Mom says all boys tell stupid jokes when they're ten."

Just then, she noticed that Uncle Gwo-Jenn was coming out of his house with Grandmother and Grandfather Lin, who lived with him and Auntie Ying-Ying. Melanie's uncle and grandparents wore their church clothes, but Cousin Connie followed them, dressed in a red Tee and her old blue coveralls. Behind her came her mother, Auntie Ying-Ying, who carried out napkins and plastic punch cups. They made a mixed ethnic picture, Melanie thought—FOB, fresh-off-the-boat, except for Cousin Connie, who dressed WTA, way-too-American.

Mom had arrived at the nearby table and was setting the basket of silverware down. "Hi, girls," she said to Melanie's guests. "We're so glad you could join us for Melanie's party. Melanie, perhaps you'd introduce us."

Heat rushed to Melanie's face. "I was just going to," she put in quickly and began the introductions.

Her parents and Silvee answered nicely and, luckily, William only said "Hi." But Uncle Gwo-Jenn and Grandmother and Grandfather Lin were formal, even bowing a little. Auntie Ying-Ying said, "I already know girls. I meet yesterday at neighborhood garage bargains and tell them come."

Connie smiled and gave them a small wave. "Hi, kids."

"Are you the famous Fender-Bender?" Jess asked.

Connie laughed. "Don't tell me my reputation is already all over the neighborhood!"

"You bent up many car already all over neighborhood," Auntie Ying-Ying joked. "Neighbors run when they see you driving!"

Everyone laughed, then Grandmother and Grandfather settled at the table.

"When we eat?" Grandfather Lin asked loudly because he didn't hear well.

"I run now . . . get egg rolls," Auntie Ying-Ying answered, then glanced at the girls. "I make two kinds egg rolls for you . . . chicken and shrimp. Two kinds."

"Ummmm . . . thank you," Becky answered. "That's nice of you, Mrs. Lin."

"You call me Auntie Ying-Ying, too!" she said, running for the door. "Connie, you come help."

"Let's sit over there," Melanie suggested, nodding at the most distant red-tiled bench at the courtyard edge. "I don't have to help today."

"Great," Jess said, and they made their way to the bench. When they sat down she asked, "I've been wondering, are you Chinese or Japanese or what?"

"American," Melanie said. "American-born Chinese. I was born in New York City."

Cara gave Jess a reproachful look. "Don't you remember, Melanie mentioned the wall out front being called 'The Great Wall of China'?"

"Ooops," Jess answered. "I forgot."

After that, no one seemed to know what to say.

Finally Melanie said, "Tell me more about the Twelve Candles Club. All I know from the TV interview is that Becky is president. What do the rest of you do?"

"Jess is vice-president, in charge of phone messages, since she has her own phone in her room," Becky explained. "Cara is secretary, since she's the writer among us. And Tricia is treasurer."

"As for what we actually do," Tricia added, "baby-sitting, of course, and Morning Fun for Kids for ages four to eight on

Monday, Wednesday, and Friday mornings in my back-yard. . . . Then sometimes we do party helping . . . dog sitting . . . light housecleaning and car washing . . . all kinds of work."

"Sounds like fun," Melanie said.

"It is," Cara told her. "I didn't know if I'd like it at first, but it's really been fun, and we've earned lots of money already this summer."

"Remember, yesterday you asked me if I'd be interested in joining?" Melanie asked. "I think I would. Mom says I'm a good worker, even if I haven't done much baby-sitting."

"What about modeling?" Tricia asked.

"I probably can't for a while." She showed them the band-age on her knee. "Not with that. Usually I'd have to be on call. But I could be a last-minute backup for the Twelve Candles Club if you need someone."

"That reminds me," Tricia said. "Tomorrow afternoon the fire department is giving a free class in baby-sitting. They're teaching CPR and all kinds of other stuff we should know. Melanie could learn about baby-sitting there."

"Maybe I could," Melanie answered. "If you really want me, I'll ask my mom. I'm not doing anything else tomorrow."

"We've talked it over since yesterday," Becky said, taking a breath. "We sure need help, but we've decided if we ask new members, it'd be best to have a trial period. You know, try them out for a while. The four of us all knew each other for ages before we started the club, but we don't know you well yet. We feel bad about it, but that does seem best."

Melanie swallowed, trying to hide her hurt. "I guess I don't blame you. You don't want some stranger coming in and ruin-ing the whole club."

She was just going to say she'd be glad to be a trial member when Tricia said, "Anyhow, we thought we should ask you to just think about it now."

That meant they weren't sure about her yet, Melanie decided. She hoped that the birthday party would go well. "Thanks. I'll think about it and ask my parents, too."

Connie came by, offering egg rolls from a tray. "Very good egg rolls," she announced, talking choppy on purpose. "Very good chicken, this side . . . very good shrimp, that side. Please, you take."

"Come on, Connie!" Melanie protested. "They'll think you're fresh off the boat." She turned to her friends. "Connie was the valedictorian of her high school class of thousands in New York. She's a brain."

One strap of her cousin's denim coveralls had fallen back off her shoulder, and she looked more like a high schooler than college-aged. "Very good egg rolls," she said, bowing and still talking stupid. "Please, you help you-self."

Each of them took an egg roll and bit in.

"Hey, it's good!" Tricia said, and the others agreed.

"Haven't you eaten egg rolls before?" Melanie asked.

It turned out that Becky and Tricia had, but Cara and Jess shook their heads. "We eat lots of Mexican food in southern California," Jess explained.

"And Italian, like pizzas and spaghetti," Becky said.

As they sat discussing different foods, Melanie wondered what Auntie Ying-Ying had prepared for dinner. She hadn't said—and sometimes she made very peculiar Chinese delicacies.

Melanie glanced up and saw a cloud of smoke rising from

the wok, and her aunt laughing and chatting as she tossed what must be meat and vegetables.

"Tell us more about modeling," Jess said.

Melanie tried to think where to begin. "Well, there's four types of models . . . the girl-next-door look, sort of like Becky with brown or blond hair, healthy and bright looking . . . the all-American look, sort of like Tricia . . . the fashion look, which is more like Cara . . . and the character look. . . ." She hesitated.

Jess laughed. "Which is more like me!"

"You said it," Melanie answered, smiling herself.

"Besides their looks, what kind of kids do they want?" Tricia asked.

"Kids with sparkle, turn-on personalities. Now that I've told you that, this sounds just the opposite, but they don't want someone who upstages the product. They want the model to make their product look great."

The girls nodded, so she guessed they understood. "For sure, they don't want kids who have bad moods or are spoiled or clingers. You have to follow instructions and not be restless. You have to be well disciplined."

"Sounds just like us," Cara joked.

"Yeah," Tricia answered with a grin.

"Modeling sounds great," Melanie told them, "but you miss out on lots of fun stuff. Like sports, dance lessons, and birthday parties. The good side, though, is you can make lots of money and it builds confidence."

"You do seem confident," Becky said.

"Not always!" Melanie replied, quite truthfully. In fact, right this very minute, she wished she felt more confident about her birthday party.

"Dinner!" Auntie Ying-Ying called out, "Please, all sit at table!" Her hair was frazzled from the smoke and steam, but it didn't stop her excitement. "All come now!"

"Come on," Melanie told them.

As the honored birthday person, she sat at the end of the long red-tiled table. To her right were Cara and Jess, and to her left, Becky and Tricia. To Melanie's relief, Connie sat next to Tricia, who would probably enjoy a pretend accent. And, luckily, William had seated himself next to Jess, who, having three brothers, would probably put up with him best. The rest of her family sat along the sides of the table without being crowded, since Mom had planned the table and benches for twenty.

Auntie Ying-Ying said, "Charlie, please you make prayer in English." She added with a grin, "I think God, He maybe understand English, too."

Melanie wanted to die, but her father nodded, smiling. "Shall we bow our heads?"

She scarcely heard the words, only that he asked a special blessing on her for her twelfth year and on her new friends. When he said, "Amen," she thought again of Auntie's fondness for peculiar delicacies.

"What are we having?" she asked as the dishes began to be passed.

"Flied lice," Connie teased.

"Come on!" Melanie protested. She looked at her bewildered friends. "Connie's being crazy. She means fried rice."

She was glad to see her friends all smile, probably with relief, and she wondered if Cousin Connie wasn't becoming more and more like Auntie Ying-Ying.

Her aunt sat at the far end of the table across from Mom,

so they could get up easily for serving. "We eat you favorite, Melanieee!" she called out. "Beef with snow pea, water chestnut. And extra for birthday, cashew-nut chicken."

"Thank you," Melanie called back. "Thanks a lot."

"And special delicacy!" her aunt added.

Not too special, Melanie hoped. She decided not to ask what the delicacy might be. She was glad to see her friends helping themselves to rice and the beef and chicken dishes. And she was glad to see that everyone had forks and knives, too, instead of chopsticks.

"Here comes the good stuff!" William announced.

"What?"

He grinned, but remained quiet as another dish came around. Connie handed it to Tricia, whose eyes widened with alarm. Without taking anything, she quickly passed the dish on to Becky, who backed away slightly. Then Melanie saw why. The dish held Grandfather Lin's all-time favorite delicacy: deep-fried duck feet.

Without saying a word, Melanie passed the dish on to Cara, whose eyes widened, too. Jess looked as if she might say something, then decided against it. Next, the dish came to William, who usually wouldn't touch them. Now, however, he made a big show of taking some.

"Duck feet . . . yum," he said so everyone would hear. "I l-o-v-e eating duck feet."

"You do not!" Melanie replied.

"Do too," he argued, and began to eat one. He didn't just eat it as others might, but made a huge production of eating the webs between the duck's toes and rolling his eyes at the toe nails. "Nice and crunchy," he remarked. "Just how I like them. Crunchy duck feet."

Even Jess, who didn't seem to be as squeamish as the other girls, was leaning away from him.

"Stop that, William!" Melanie warned. "It's sickening, not to mention disgusting." She wished that Mom or Dad could hear, but they were too far down the table and speaking with Grandmother and Grandfather Lin.

"I l-o-v-e duck feet," William announced again.

Melanie drew a deep breath.

"Ignore him," she told the girls, though her own stomach was churning. "It's a wonder he doesn't want soy sauce on it."

"Good idea," William answered, reaching for the soy sauce bottle. "It'll make these poor orange duck feet want to waddle again."

"Stop it!" Melanie muttered. "Stop it right now!"

Her new friends smiled uneasily, but Melanie noticed that they didn't eat much, either.

"Do we get fortune cookies for dessert?" Becky asked.

"I don't think so," Melanie answered, but she was thinking, *I sure hope not!* "You get them in Chinese restaurants, not very often in homes. They're actually American."

Finally, the main course was over, and she was glad to see her mother bring out a bakery-made birthday cake with blazing candles. Connie and William had already piled the birthday presents on the table. Right in front of her, he'd put what looked like his present—a shoe box wrapped in silvery kitchen foil. In fact, he stood behind his place on the bench watching it.

"Happy birthday to you . . ." they began singing as Mom approached with the candlelit chocolate-frosted cake.

As they sang, Melanie noticed that the shoe box lid had tiny breathing holes punched in it! What's more, the lid was wrapped separately—and it was moving!

Suddenly the entire foiled shoe box gave a huge jerk!

Becky reared back. "Yiii!" she shrieked in the midst of the birthday singing.

Just then the lid of the shoe box lifted, and a huge gray lizard, wearing silver-foil zigzaggy humps like a dragon, began to emerge.

The girls jumped away from the table, shrieking.

"Announcement! Announcement!" William yelled, grinning. "Honorable Chinese dragon come to party! Honorable Chinese dragon!"

Melanie turned to him and shouted, "William Lin . . . I'm going to get you for this!" It was just like him to ruin her party.

But when she turned back to her guests, she saw them begin to snicker. The rest of the family laughed and kept on singing as the lizard moved across the table. "Happy birthday, dear Melanie . . ."

Suddenly firecrackers crackled and banged right behind her, making her and her friends jump again.

William!

"Yikes!" Jess yelled.

" . . . happy birthday to you!" they all finished, then started laughing. All except Melanie.

It hasn't been that happy so far! she thought as they began the "many more birthdays." Her new friends must think that her family . . . and being Chinese . . . were crazy!

She tried to smile anyhow.

As for "many more birthdays," things just had to get better in her twelfth year, that was all!

CHAPTER

4

*A*fter breakfast, the first thing Melanie had to do was to phone her modeling agent, Ms. Schivitz. It was a real shame that things had gone wrong before she'd done a single job for the agency. She glanced down at her scraped knee, where the big bandage still clung.

Feeling too embarrassed to tell about the skateboard accident, Melanie had already practiced her explanation in her head. She kept it brief as she spoke on the kitchen phone. "I'm sorry to let you know that I fell and skinned my knee, Ms. Schivitz. I knew you'd want to be told that I can't do any modeling with both knees showing, at least not for a while."

"Not very professional of you," her new agent remarked, her tone chilly. "Not one bit professional, if you ask me."

Melanie felt her mouth dropping open, and she rushed on. "But I always called my agency in New York as soon as I knew I couldn't work. I thought you'd want the same—"

Ms. Schivitz interrupted. "What you have to be very clear about if you wish to work for this agency is this: I don't consider it very professional of you to be out playing and skinning your knee. Do you understand?"

Melanie's hand clutched the phone tightly. "Yes, Ms. Schivitz. I wasn't playing, though. It was more of a . . . a freak accident—"

"Never mind the excuses," her agent replied. "I have another call. Goodbye, Melanie!"

Melanie stood staring at the phone's receiver in her hand. Her new agent hadn't even said to call when her knee was fine again. In New York, Melanie Lin had been considered a valuable professional model, but she sure wasn't important or even considered professional in Santa Rosita, California!

Mom passed through the kitchen, carrying her artist's easel. "What's wrong?"

"Ms. Schivitz wasn't at all pleased about my knee. She thought I'd been playing and said it wasn't professional. . . ." Melanie felt like crying. Between the embarrassment at her birthday party yesterday and now her agent's coldness! But she wouldn't cry . . . she wouldn't. . . !

Raising her nicely arched brows, Mom asked, "You really didn't need this on top of everything else, did you?"

Tears flooded her eyes, and Melanie shook her head.

"I'm sorry if William embarrassed you with his 'honorable Chinese dragon' and the firecrackers yesterday. Dad spoke with him last night and told him to be more thoughtful, especially in front of your friends."

Melanie blinked hard. "Thanks."

Her mom rubbed Melanie's shoulders comfortingly. "Anyhow, your friends seemed to enjoy the party. They told Auntie

Ying-Ying and me several times about how much they enjoyed everything."

"That's only because they've got better manners than William," Melanie answered. "Lots better! Why can't he be nicer like Silvee?"

"Because ten-year-old boys are often a nuisance, and five-year-old girls are usually fairly nice. I hear even your father was a pest at ten."

"You're kidding."

Mom shook her head, her dark eyes shining at the thought of it. "Grandmother Lin says he was full of mischief. And you know very well that he can still be lots of fun."

Melanie remembered her father putting a hand to his mouth to hide his laughter when the "honorable Chinese dragon" got loose. And he hadn't even hid his laugh when the firecrackers had gone off and they'd all jumped. But he would never intentionally embarrass her. He was careful about that.

She drew a deep breath. "If Dad used to be like that, maybe there's hope for William."

"Let's believe it and expect it," Mom answered, "though the Chinese dragon was rather funny, and the firecrackers certainly added excitement. I'm sure that William considered his part in your party a great success."

"Well, I didn't! And I didn't appreciate Connie talking crazy Chinese, or Auntie Ying-Ying being so . . . you know, enthusiastic."

Mom smiled. "You mean your aunt was her usual self?"

Melanie nodded. "Yeah, she was her usual self."

Mom gave a little laugh. "Most families have at least one eccentric member, and Auntie Ying-Ying is a wonderful one."

"Yeah, I guess."

"At least your new friends invited you to go to the baby-sitting class today," Mom said. "They must like you, despite William and Connie and your dear aunt."

"I don't know about that."

"I'm sure they do. How could anyone *not* like you?"

"Easy," Melanie answered. She didn't even like herself in the mood she was in now. Besides, they hadn't invited her this morning to Tricia's house to help with Morning Fun for Kids. She'd heard the little kids laughing and yelling all the way up in her room.

"You know Auntie Ying-Ying is one of the most good-hearted people on this earth," Mom said. "She wore herself out to give you a nice dinner."

"I know it."

On top of everything else, Melanie felt guilty. "I'll go to her house in a minute and see if I can help," she decided. "There's probably still dishes and pots and pans to clean up."

"That'd be nice, Mel. It's soothing to wash dishes with another person; it seems to smooth troubles away. Besides, it'd put some distance between you and William this morning. And this afternoon you'll be out at that baby-sitting class, too." Mom picked up her easel. "Silvee and I are going to paint— and color—in the backyard, so we'll be around."

"William's already out in the backyard," Melanie said. "I heard him bellow his kung fu yell for the whole neighborhood. I'm just glad I didn't have to sit with him for breakfast."

Mom gave her another pat on the shoulder, then picked up her easel. "Sometime this summer I'd like you to pose for a portrait for me."

"Me pose for you? No way! You'll turn me into all planes and angles like your abstract paintings."

"I'll make you just as sweet and lovely as you are," her mother answered. She gave her a bright smile, then let herself out the side door.

Minutes later, Melanie made her way through the courtyard, then knocked on Auntie Ying-Ying's kitchen door.

"Come in! Come in!" Auntie called over a rattle of pots and pans. "You know you no need knock on door."

Melanie let herself into the red and white kitchen. "I thought maybe I could help you finish washing the dishes."

"You want help wash dishes?" Auntie Ying-Ying asked, blinking with surprise. She wore an old black Chinese blouse and slacks, and stood over the sink with soapy arms.

Melanie nodded. "You worked so hard for my party."

"My honor . . . it was my honor," Auntie insisted. "You know I do anything for you, Melanieee. Anything!!!!"

Melanie nodded sheepishly and grabbed a dishcloth. "I know it. Where's everyone else?"

"You uncle, he take Connie Fender-Bender to try for driver's license."

"How could I forget?!"

"Grandmother and Grandfather Lin go for good laugh."

Melanie had to smile.

Connie had been practicing driving every day for a month. So far, she'd bashed her red car into the garage workbench on one end and the garage door on the other. She'd knocked down her parents' mailbox and rammed into a fireplug, setting off a gusher. The fire department had roared up in a red engine to turn the water off.

Drying a mixing bowl, Melanie said, "Let's hope she hasn't hit any cars."

"Uuuuhhhhh, don't say . . . don't even think! I praying

and praying she not hit cars, and we all live through Connie's driving. I never ride with her! She make me too nervous!"

They both laughed at the thought of her being even more nervous, and Auntie Ying-Ying threw her soapy arms around Melanie. After a moment, she said, "Oh, Melanieee, you are a good girl to come and help your old auntie now."

Melanie smiled at her aunt, but she felt like an imposter, not a good girl at all.

"Hey-hey, Melanie, let's g-o-o-o-o! Let's g-o-o-o-o!"

"Coming!" She pushed the garage door opener, then jumped on her bike and rode out. It was a wonderful sight to have Jess, Cara, Becky, and Tricia on their bikes waiting for her on the driveway. They wore colorful shorts and Tees, and Melanie was glad she'd worn her coral shorts and top, although the bandage on her knee was definitely not a happy sight.

"Hey-hey, yourselves, you guys look great!"

They all grinned, and she hoped that today at the baby-sitters' class everything would go right.

From somewhere inside, Silvee called out, "I'm closing the garage door for you, Melanie!"

"Thanks, Silvee!"

"Have a good time!" Silvee yelled. "Have a good time!"

"Silvee is cute," Becky remarked as they rode their bikes through the cul-de-sac. "My sister Amanda is five, too. Trouble is, with Mom working, Amanda's usually with Gram at her place near the beach. Maybe we can get them together Saturday."

"Oh-oh, watch out!" Melanie exclaimed, seeing Connie's red car come down the street. "Here's my cousin! Pedal for your lives!"

She was glad to see that Cousin Connie had on the car's blinker to turn left into the cul-de-sac. She was driving very slowly, and her lips were turned down like the cartoon of a very unhappy face.

"Did you get your license?" Melanie called out as the car pulled even with them.

Uncle Gwo-Jenn had rolled down his passenger-side window. "No license. Fender-Bender backed car into Department of Motor Vehicle's fence. Only knock down a little. She tries again in a few weeks."

"You're teasing!"

Her uncle shook his head, and Connie wasn't talking, which probably was best when she was driving. It was hard to believe that Connie could get all A's in school but couldn't pass a driver's test.

"See you later!"

Melanie pedaled harder to catch up with her friends. They'd all heard her uncle, so she jabbered, "I can't believe it! Connie's such a brain, but she can't figure out driving. I can't believe it . . . I can't!"

"It's strange all right," Jess said. "I guess some people have trouble learning to drive, but I don't plan to be one of them!" She rose up to pedal harder and lead them up the street.

Melanie was glad to see Cara was waiting for her to catch up, and they set off riding side by side.

"I had a good time at your party," Cara said shyly. "It was. . . ." She hesitated, searching for the right word.

Melanie felt nervous—and jabbery. "Unusual? Peculiar? Weird? Strange?"

"Unusual," Cara replied, "but interesting and nice."

Melanie felt better, hearing Cara's answer. Maybe it'd be

better to say something about the weird stuff in her family since she'd already jabbered.

"*Especially unusual* was my 'honorable Chinese dragon' lizard from William . . . not to mention his making such a big deal about eating the duck feet," she said.

Smiling a little, Cara pedaled along beside her. "The lizard was funny. Wish I'd had a video camera to get pictures of us shrieking and jumping up from the table. It's the kind of stuff that's fun to see later on."

"How about the duck feet?"

"Never mind that!" Cara answered. "Though it would probably be great for seeing in a picture later, too."

Later would be soon enough to see pictures of any of it, Melanie thought. But talking about things did seem to be better than pretending they had never happened.

"They eat lizards in some places in Mexico," Cara said.

"You're kidding!" Melanie exclaimed.

Cara shook her head. "Nope. They eat big ugly lizards called iguanas."

"I didn't know that."

"You do now," Cara answered. "I guess if Mexican people can eat lizards, there's no reason why others can't eat duck feet . . . even if it is surprising to see."

Melanie was glad to hear it, though she didn't know what the rest of them thought. "I guess you must be Mexican— yipes, excuse me. I mean Hispanic."

"Half," Cara answered. "My father's Hispanic, if you didn't guess from a name like Hernandez." Cara smiled. "But just in case you're wondering, I don't eat lizards."

Melanie smiled back. "I don't eat duck feet, either."

"But it wouldn't be terrible if we did eat them, would it?"

"I guess not." It struck Melanie that Cara had given some thought to ethnic differences, maybe more than she had herself.

They grinned at each other and rode on.

On Ocean Avenue, they turned right, riding single file into the bike lane. Melanie rode last in line, reminding herself that although she might feel better now—even a little accepted by Cara—she was still on trial.

From what she'd heard so far, she knew this: The Twelve Candles Club had been Becky's idea, and they used Jess's phone, and Morning Fun for Kids took place in Tricia's yard. They were the ones in charge, not Cara Hernandez. But the most important thing to remember was that Melanie Lin was *not-not-not* a member of the Twelve Candles Club. At least not yet.

When they arrived at the Santa Rosita Fire Station, two big fire engines and an ambulance stood out front, and there were already nine or ten other girls waiting for the class to begin. A friendly fireman greeted them. "Bikes locked up in the bike rack," he said. "Baby-sitting class starts at exactly two o'clock. There's lots to discuss."

Two gray-and-white cats nosed around the outside of the white firehouse. A big old dalmatian dog cast a sleepy glance at them, then closed his eyes and drowsed again.

As they parked their bikes in the bike rack, Jess asked Melanie, "Do Chinese people eat dogs?"

"No way!" Melanie answered in shock. "At least not us."

"I heard some Asian people do," Jess explained as she fastened her bike lock.

"Not us!" Melanie repeated. Hearing herself sound so defensive, she quickly joked, "We don't even eat dragons."

Jess grinned. "I guess not. Anyhow, they're imaginary creatures. So why are Chinese people interested in them?"

"Probably old superstitions," Melanie answered, locking her bike in the bike rack with theirs. "Some of the old Chinese are very superstitious."

She tried to sound composed as she added, "My family doesn't believe in fire-breathing monsters. Mostly dragons are for fun in Chinese New Year parades." There was no sense in saying that some in her family, like Auntie Ying-Ying, might once have believed in dragons.

"Come *on*, Jess!" Tricia warned. "That's enough questions!"

Jess wobbled her head comically. "Well, I like to know things. What's wrong with asking? She asked about Jewish people at Sunday school."

Melanie guessed there'd be lots more questions. Why couldn't they just accept her as Melanie Elizabeth Lin, an American-born Chinese girl, just like she was?

Besides, being a model made her special, didn't it?

CHAPTER

5

Melanie rode her bike down Ocean Avenue, single file behind Jess, Becky, Tricia, and Cara. The fire department's baby-sitting class had been informative, and she'd learned more about caring for kids than she hoped to ever use.

Behind her, her bike rack held handouts like "Basic First Aid," "Guide for Baby-sitters," "Baby-sitter's Emergency Checklist," and "A Baby-Sitter's Guide to Keeping Kids Safe."

They'd practiced changing diapers on baby-sized plastic dolls, and had even practiced CPR, using the dolls to learn how to breathe into the mouth and pump the chest of a kid who'd stopped breathing. It'd all been easy for Tricia and Becky, but harder for Jess and Cara, who had no younger brothers or sisters. But, as baby-sitting went, Melanie most definitely knew the least.

On the corner of La Crescenta, they waited for the green light, then pedaled across Ocean Avenue and onto their street.

As usual, there was almost no traffic.

Tricia's reddish blond hair blew in the afternoon breeze as she rode up alongside Melanie. "I've been thinking about your not having references," she said, a little embarrassed. "You may not have any from baby-sitting, but I'll bet you do from modeling."

"Hey, I do!" Melanie answered. "My New York agency wrote a letter for me to take to agencies here. You want a copy?"

"It'd be more businesslike," Becky answered, pedaling along and nodding. "The rest of us had a conference while you were giving CPR to your plastic baby. Why don't you bring your reference to our meeting at Jess's house at four-thirty? You could sit in on the meeting and see if you're still interested in joining the club. And Jess wants to invite you—" She stopped, turning back. "Here she comes now."

Invite me to what? Melanie wondered eagerly.

Jess rode up on the other side. "We're having pizzas and a slumber party after the meeting at my house. Think you could come for the night?"

"You mean to the meeting and to the slumber party, too?"

"Sure," Jess answered, grinning. "Don't worry. We talked it all over."

Whoa! Melanie thought. *They may not have invited me to Morning Fun for Kids this morning, but they've just asked me to their meeting—and to a slumber party!*

Best not to seem too excited. "Probably I can," she answered. "I'll ride straight home and pick up the letter from my New York agency, then I can ask Mom if I can come for the slumber party, too."

"Be sure to bring your sleeping bag and your swimsuit!"

Jess told her. "We have a pool."

"I will!" Melanie answered, forgetting to hide her excitement. They were just at her cul-de-sac, so she pedaled off, jabbering a "See you guys later . . . I mean *soon*, I hope! Thanks a lot! See you!"

She rode up the sidewalk and, hearing voices, curved onto the grass behind "The Great Wall of China." Sure enough, her mother was reading a book to Silvee as they sat on one of the benches. "I thought I heard you," Melanie said.

"There's Melanie!" Silvee exclaimed, jumping up. "Melanie. . . ! Melanie. . . !"

Melanie braked her bike and hopped off on the grass. "You'll never ever guess what! I've been invited to a Twelve Candles Club meeting—and then to stay for pizza and a slumber party at Jess's house. Can I . . . I mean, *may* I go?"

Silvee's dark eyes widened with excitement, and Mom looked pleased, too. "You may. All you'll miss here is Auntie's leftovers from your party."

"Thanks! I have to hurry. I need a copy of the letter of recommendation from New York and my sleeping bag and my jammies. The new summer ones, I guess."

"A copy of the recommendation?" Mom asked.

Melanie propped her bike against a courtyard post and started for the side door of her house. "They want to be businesslike . . . you know, *careful* about admitting new members to the club."

Mom raised her brows. "I see. Well, I put extra copies in that folder in your bottom desk drawer."

"Thanks!"

Melanie hurried to the side door and raced upstairs to her room. First, she took out a copy of the letter from her New

York agency and read it quickly to be sure it was as good as she'd remembered.

> *To Whomever It May Concern:*
>
> *Melanie Elizabeth Lin is one of our foremost preteen models. She is reliable, agreeable, and very professional. We have received nothing but praise from the agencies and photographers with whom she has worked in the past eight years. We are sorry to lose her.*
>
> Sincerely,

It was signed by the famous Wilhemina de Haan herself, which was very impressive for people who knew about New York modeling. Unfortunately, she suspected it had only served to make Ms. Schivitz jealous and even resentful.

But at least the Twelve Candles Club would see that she'd been considered reliable, agreeable, and very professional, Melanie decided, laying the letter on her bed. The letter was proof that she'd been a New York model, just like the photos of her on her walls.

As she rushed for her closet, she fleetingly noticed her birthday gifts piled on the window seat—a stuffed brown bear from Jess, a book named *Summer Promises* from Cara, nice hair ornaments from Tricia, and a glass jewelry box from Becky. She was still amazed that they had given her presents when they'd been asked at the last moment and had hardly known her.

She grabbed her modeling carry-all bag from the closet and plopped it on her bed. Instead of scurrying about to pack things, she jotted down a list like she'd done for modeling jobs. Lists were very important to keep from forgetting things for a job or leaving stuff behind.

toothbrush
toothpaste
jammies
white shorts
purple Tee
white thongs (to use as slippers too)
sleeping bag
swimsuit

She glanced at her watch. No time for a shower or washing her hair. Best to take shampoo for after the swim.

In the bathroom she shared with Silvee, she grabbed a small tube of shampoo. She'd just change into her jean shorts and white Aztec Tee. Oops, add bandages to the list!

She doubted that her knee had gotten any better from the bicycle ride to the fire station. Well, no time now! She'd check it out after she'd been swimming.

Melanie arrived at Jess's two-story white stucco house a few minutes before four-thirty, arriving just as Cara crossed the street from her house.

"Hey, I'm glad you're here," Cara said, her brown eyes warm and welcoming. She was juggling her sleeping bag, a carry-on case, and a notebook. "I hope you get into the club."

"Thanks!" Melanie answered. Since Cara was half Hispanic, Melanie wondered if that meant Cara would be glad not to be the *only* ethnic type in the club.

She felt as if she should say something, but not about getting into the club. "You look great in white," she remarked about Cara's white shorts and top outfit.

"Thanks," Cara answered, pleased. "I wear a lot of it."

"I do, too. White is good on 'winters.' "

Cara gave her such a blank look that Melanie added, "You know, 'winters' are people with dark hair and dark eyes."

"Oh," Cara answered.

"We look best in cool, clear colors," Melanie explained into the silence. "And we're the only ones who can wear black and pure white well."

"I guess models have to know things like that," Cara said.

Melanie nodded, hoping she hadn't seemed boastful. "They do. If only the advertisers paid attention to our colors." She wished now that she'd never brought up the subject.

Cara pounded out a *knock-knock, knock-knock-knock-knock* at the door, then explained, "Jess's room used to be a three-car garage, so it has this outside door. She keeps it locked now, ever since the robber arrived at her last slumber party."

Melanie remembered reading about it in the newspaper. "I'll bet!"

Jess threw open the door to her huge room. "All right! Everybody's here now! Put your stuff on the corner mat and come have a seat. The phone's been ringing like mad already. People are beginning to call early to get ahead of the pack."

Melanie glanced over and saw Becky on the phone and Tricia chalking up something on the greenboard over Jess's desk. In that corner, the room had a twin bed corner unit, an old trunk, a chest of drawers, and a desk. But the rest of the room held blue floor mats, a small trampoline, a gymnast's beam and vaulting horse, a ballet barre in front of a huge mirror, and, on the high walls, huge posters of Olympic gymnasts.

She must have seemed surprised, because Jess said, "Forgot to tell you I'm a gymnast."

"I guess so!" Melanie said, still glancing around.

Jess laughed. "Anyhow, come over and have a seat on the beds."

Melanie followed Cara and put her carry-all bag and sleeping bag on the corner mat, then remembered the agency letter and took it out of the carry-all. "When do you want my letter of recommendation?"

"I guess during the meeting—if we have a chance to get started with so many phone calls," Jess said. She led the way to the twin bed corner. "Everyone in Santa Rosita must be going out this week and needing baby-sitters."

Melanie sat down on the bed just as Becky hung up the phone. "Phew! Five calls on the machine while we were at the fire station and three calls here already."

"Let's keep the phone off the hook so we can get the meeting going," Tricia suggested. "I make a motion we keep the phone off the hook—"

Becky rolled her blue eyes. "We haven't even started the meeting yet, you wacko!"

"Ooops!" Tricia said and put a hand to her mouth. "I *am* going wacko, all right." Turning, she called out, "Hey, Cara and Melanie!"

Melanie gave her a good smile and said, "Hi," to her and Becky. This was one time Jabberwacky Melanie was not going to j-a-b-b-e-r and make a fool of herself.

Becky grabbed Jess's wooden desk chair and sat down on it backwards. "This meeting of the Twelve Candles Club will now come to order," she said, pounding the back of the chair for emphasis. She smiled at Melanie, who had plopped down next to Cara on a bed. "We are glad to welcome Melanie Lin as a guest to this meeting."

"Thank you," Melanie said as calmly as she could.

"The secretary will now read the minutes of the last meeting," Becky announced.

Cara stood up, notebook in hand, and began to read. "The last meeting of the Twelve Candles Club took place on Friday, July 12, at four-thirty. After the reading of the minutes of the last meeting by Cara Hernandez and the treasurer's report by Tricia Bennett, we had old business. This was mainly about having too many job offers and not enough members. We talked about not taking too many jobs or we'd start to hate working." Cara caught a breath, then read on. "During the new business, we discussed the jobs we would take and did all of the scheduling. Respectfully submitted, Cara Hernandez."

She closed the notebook and sat down on the bed with Melanie again.

"May we now have the treasurer's report?" Becky asked.

Tricia hopped up and read from her notebook, "The treasury of the Twelve Candles Club has $18.87. There are no bills to pay. The latest expenses were for graham crackers, raisin packs, and orange juice for Morning Fun for Kids. We have plenty of money for the next few days' expenses. Respectfully submitted, Tricia Bennett."

Tricia settled on the twin bed across from them, and Jess plopped down on the floor to do leg stretches.

"Any old business?" Becky asked.

There wasn't any.

"Any new business?"

"Yes!" Jess said. "Let's not forget that we're keeping this Wednesday afternoon open to go to the beach."

"Noted," Becky said. "Any other new business?"

Melanie handed her letter of recommendation to Becky, who took it out of the envelope. "Okay if I read this aloud?"

"Sure," Melanie answered.

Becky read, "To Whomever It May Concern: Melanie Elizabeth Lin is one of our foremost preteen models. She is reliable, agreeable, and very professional. We have received nothing but praise from the agencies and photographers with whom she has worked in the past eight years. We are sorry to lose her. Sincerely, Wilhemina de Haan, de Haan Modeling Agency, New York, New York."

"Wow," Jess said, "that really sounds good."

Tricia nodded, impressed. "It does."

It did sound good, Melanie thought, though the words "preteen model" had jumped out at this reading of it. One of the problems of being a preteen model was growing out of sample sizes, and she'd been growing like crazy ever since Christmas. What if she outgrew the sample sizes soon? But there was no sense saying anything about it to her new friends.

Becky told Cara, "Please note that a good letter of recommendation was read about Melanie Lin. She was called reliable, agreeable, and very professional."

Becky turned to Melanie. "Is it all right for us to keep the letter in our recommendation folder?"

Melanie nodded. "Yes, it's just a copy."

"Thank you," Becky said. "As I told Melanie, we will need recommendations from any new girls interested in joining the club. I also told her about our trial period."

Jess broke in, "If she makes it through a Morning Fun for Kids, she should make it through anything, no sweat! Can we invite her for Wednesday morning?"

"I make a motion that we invite her for Morning Fun for Kids on Wednesday morning," Cara said.

Tricia added, "I second the motion." She glanced at Melanie. "The Funners will love you!"

"Funners?"

"That's what we call the kids who come," Tricia explained.

When they voted, all four hands shot up, and Melanie smiled with relief. If she did a good job, maybe she'd get into the club.

"Any other new business besides taking the phone calls and dividing them up?" Becky asked.

Tricia waved her hand in the air.

"Yes, Tricia?" Becky asked.

"I'm running out of theme ideas for the magic carpet ride for Morning Fun for Kids. We've done cowboys, circus, flying, pirates, and all kinds of other stuff. I thought maybe some of you would have suggestions."

They all stared at each other.

Suddenly Jess stopped her leg stretches. "Whoa, I have an idea. With Melanie there, maybe we could do a Chinese theme . . . you know, a Chinese New Year's parade like they show on TV with make-believe dragons and stuff."

Melanie pressed her lips together, wishing they'd thought of almost anything else. Why did they always have to see her as so different?

"Melanie," Becky asked, "what do you think about it?"

"It's . . . it's all right, I guess. But I don't know anything about the . . . magic carpet rides."

"We roll out an old rug on the lawn, then the kids sit on it and close their eyes, and we go for imaginary rides to interesting places," Tricia explained. "You know, like a dude ranch or the moon. Just-for-fun places."

"So you'd want to do a Chinese New Year's parade?"

Tricia rolled her green eyes thoughtfully. "It might work.

We have a record of music from the *Flower Drum Song* . . . but what would we use for a huge dragon? Let's face it, my raggedy brown rug and bed sheets aren't enough." She turned to Melanie. "Do you have any ideas?"

Melanie did, but she felt reluctant to tell it. On the other hand, she did want to be in the club. "My aunt has a big plastic dragon head she bought when she worked at the New York Chinese Cultural Association. We thought she was crazy to bring it all the way to California, but she said there'd be Chinese New Year's Day celebrations here, too."

"Is it valuable?" Tricia asked. "I know how much some costumes and props cost."

"Probably not too valuable," Melanie said, since Auntie Ying-Ying was super thrifty. "She didn't buy it new."

"We'd be very careful with it," Becky promised. "But that still doesn't give us the rest of the dragon."

"Whoa!" Tricia exclaimed. "We could use those big green plastic garbage bags! You know how they come in rolls to tear apart. We just wouldn't tear them apart, and the kids could get under them and hold them up as we wound around the yard. And we could do a takeoff on the Siamese cat song. You know, 'I am Chi-a-nese, if you please . . .' And to eat, maybe Mom would make something with rice . . . yeah . . . rice pudding."

Rice pudding! Melanie thought, appalled.

"It's sounding better and better!" Becky exclaimed. "We'd have to be careful that little kids didn't suffocate under the plastic bags, though."

"I guess!" Jess put in. "I think we have some old dark green bed sheets. That'd be safer than plastic bags around little kids."

"Good," Tricia said. "Hey, guys! Looks like we're set for another magic carpet ride. We'd better finish the meeting so we can take calls again."

Melanie felt nervous about them doing a Chinese parade. As for something Chinese to eat, it sure wasn't rice pudding. But she had to smile in spite of herself. Kids were bound to like rice pudding lots better than fried duck feet!

CHAPTER

6

As soon as Becky replaced the phone on the receiver, it began to ring again. She picked it up and answered, "Twelve Candles Club. Oh . . . hello, Mrs. Davis."

She listened, staring at the white ceiling, then spoke loudly enough for all of them to hear. "You say it's an emergency? You need someone to sit the twins tomorrow evening from seven to ten? Thanks for asking us. We'll call you back as soon as possible."

When Becky hung up, she shook her head. "I'm already working tomorrow night."

"I'm working, too," Tricia put in.

"No way will I take care of those wild twins," Jess stated. Sitting on the white carpet between her corner twin-bed unit, she did another leg stretch. "Remember when those two went riding down the LeRoys' driveway on an office chair with that big poodle pulling them?"

"Do I remember?!" Tricia answered. "It's tattooed on my brain cells! I had to catch them! I've never run so fast in all of my life."

They all laughed, and Jess said, "Anyhow, I'm booked for tomorrow night, too."

"I'll take them," Cara said, "but only because I need the money. I'll call Mrs. Davis now."

While Cara spoke on the phone, Tricia chalked up the information under *Baby-sitting* for *Tuesday* on the greenboard over Jess's desk.

Mrs. Davis
577–0987
Sit for Jojo & Jimjim
Tues. 7–10
(Cara)

Melanie noticed that, compared to the other weekday evenings on the board, Tuesday was very full.

The moment Cara hung up the phone, it rang again.

"Twelve Candles Club," Becky said. It sounded as if it was someone she knew, and Becky told her that they'd call back. When she put down the phone, she rolled her eyes. "It's another sitting job for tomorrow evening. Mrs. Conway. I thought about saying we were all busy, but she could turn into a good client, and she might find another sitter."

The room was silent for a moment, then Tricia asked Becky, "Are you thinking what I'm thinking?"

They both glanced at Melanie, who suddenly felt rooted to the bed where she sat.

"Right on," Jess said. "It's a good time for Melanie to try it. The Conway baby is six months old now and Jason is always right there, forever telling you what to do."

67

"Me. . . ?" Melanie asked.

They nodded.

"Only if you want to," Becky said. "The baby will probably be sleeping, and you'll just have to peek into the nursery now and then. Jason is six years old, and he always knows what to do anyhow. Besides, you've had the baby-sitting class now, and you have a five-year-old sister."

They were all looking at her and waiting for her answer. If she wanted to join the Twelve Candles Club, Melanie decided, she'd better take the job now.

"Sure," she managed. "I'll have to call my mom for permission."

A minute later, Mom had said yes. As Melanie put the phone down, she asked, "You want me to call Mrs. Conway back?"

"I'll call to explain about you," Becky said, "then I'll put you on for the details." She picked up the phone and began to dial.

Melanie got up uneasily and made her way back to the phone.

As soon as it was answered, Becky said, "Hello, Mrs. Conway. This is Becky Hamilton from the Twelve Candles Club calling you back. We have a . . . umm . . . trial member who can take your job. Her name is Melanie Lin, and she is reliable, agreeable, and has just taken the fire department's baby-sitting class with us this afternoon. She lives right across the cul-de-sac from Tricia and me, too."

She listened for a moment. "Oh, yes, she's got a five-year-old sister and a ten-year-old brother herself. Okay. Fine. Here she is now for the details."

Melanie took the phone uneasily. "Hello, Mrs. Conway. This is Melanie Lin."

"Hello, Melanie," a pleasant voice said in her ear. "I'd like you to sit for us Tuesday from seven to ten-thirty. Little Pauline will be in her crib, and Jason will already have eaten dinner and just needs a story."

"Fine," Melanie said, though she did not feel in the least fine about it.

"Good," Mrs. Conway answered. "Mr. Conway will pick you up at ten till seven, and drive you home, too. What's your address?"

While Melanie told her, she hunted wildly for a pencil and paper on Jess's desk, and finally found them to write down the time and details.

"See you Tuesday, Melanie, at ten till seven."

"Yes, see you Tuesday," Melanie answered. She'd spoken the words easily, but inside she was quaking. What if something went wrong?

As she put the phone down, the rest of them grinned at her. "Now you'll have actual paid experience," Tricia said.

"I guess so," Melanie answered. "I guess I will."

She saw that Tricia was already chalking it up under *Babysitting* for *Tuesday* on the greenboard with the others.

Mrs. Conway
577–3231
Sit for Pauline and Jason
Tues. 7–10:30
(Melanie)

Written on the board, it looked official. Her trial club membership was beginning right now. If only she felt better about it . . . if only she were sure she wouldn't have to use CPR or other emergency first aid her first time out. It was too scary to even consider.

The phone rang again, this time for party helping. The next call was for car washing Saturday morning, then there were more for baby-sitting. Fortunately, the girls didn't ask her to take any more jobs.

"Were you scared when you did your first modeling job?" Tricia asked her.

Melanie shook her head, certain that Tricia had guessed how nervous she felt about her first sitting job. "I was only four years old, and Mom was modeling with me back then. I probably didn't even know what I was doing." She almost jabbered on, but caught herself.

"I didn't know your mom did modeling, too," Cara said.

Melanie nodded. "She did for a while, but she's really an artist. She decided she'd rather have a bigger family and use her spare time painting. Besides, it's harder to get good modeling jobs when you're older."

The phone interrupted, then rang again and again. Mostly the jobs were for later in the week and the weekend. Finally, just after five-thirty, the phone stopped ringing.

"Whew," Jess said, "we made it again. Let's fill out our daily planners, then have a swim before my brothers come home and take over the pool."

Melanie didn't have a daily planner like the rest of them to write her jobs into, but she was certain she wouldn't forget. Tomorrow night for Mrs. Conway from seven to ten-thirty. Melanie fervently hoped that Mrs. Conway would cancel . . . that they'd have to leave town . . . or something else would come up!

Minutes later, they were changing into their bathing suits

in the outdoor dressing rooms by the pool.

"Last one in is a toad!" Jess yelled and dived in.

"You're a toad yourself!" Tricia shouted back and dived in after her.

Melanie felt only a little better about swimming than she did about baby-sitting. She'd taken swimming lessons in New York, but there'd been too few private pools nearby, and she'd been busy modeling. As she started down the pool steps, she hoped she wouldn't make a worse fool of herself.

They pulled themselves out of the pool an hour later, and Melanie realized that between the swimming and splashing, she'd really had fun. Jess's brothers, who were all older and mostly handsome, had come in swimming for a while. They'd teased them a little, but they'd been all right. Besides, it was a big pool and a big backyard with a hill behind it covered with purple ice plant, just like behind her house.

Jess's mother stuck her head out the sliding glass door. "Pizza outside or inside, girls?"

"Are the guys staying home or not?" Jess asked her.

"Mostly not," her mom answered.

"Let's eat out here, then," Jess decided. "At the glass-topped table. You want us to help?"

"Maybe bring out the glasses, lemonade pitcher, paper plates, silverware, and salad. I'll have the pizzas out of the oven in a minute."

They dried off with beach towels, then trooped through the sliding glass door into the southwestern-style white, tan, salmon, and turquoise family room. Melanie felt like a stranger, but Mrs. McColl was friendly. Mr. McColl, an airline pilot, wasn't home. He was flying somewhere.

It only took the five of them one trip to carry out the things to the glass-topped table. Jess remarked to Melanie, "It's not as big as your outdoor table."

"I guess not," Melanie replied, since this only seated six people. "But it's big enough for us."

It occurred to her that everything here was different than her family's courtyard behind the Great Wall. And now she had to replace her bandage, since it'd come loose from swimming. Her knee didn't look a lot better, either, but it was cleaner than after she'd fallen on the asphalt.

She grabbed her carry-all and got out the new bandage. Turning away so the others wouldn't have to watch, she sat down and replaced it.

"Here's the first pizza," Mrs. McColl announced, bringing it out and putting it on the table. "It's a Morelli's special with pepperoni, mushrooms, and extra cheese. And all sliced for you to dig in."

They grinned at each other, then took slices, the cheese stringing out on the way to their plates.

"Oops!" Everyone looked up, and Jess said, "I almost forgot again! Tricia, will you say grace?"

Surprised, Melanie bowed her head with them. When she'd been at slumber parties in New York, there'd been no praying. Of course, some of her ABC friends' families were Buddhists, but they hadn't prayed, either.

Tricia kept the prayer short, and moments later, they dug in.

As she took her first bite of the thick, juicy pizza, Melanie realized that she was beginning to feel at home with them. She'd gone through a lot—the skateboard disaster, the youth group meeting, her very-Chinese birthday party, the baby-sitting class, and the club meeting. She smiled over her slice of pizza at Jess, who gave her a friendly grin back. The others were smiling at her too, Melanie realized.

Now, if she could make it through the baby-sitting and a Chinese dragon act for Morning Fun for Kids, she might really fit into the Twelve Candles Club.

She'd no more than thought it when Jess said to her, "Hey, tell us about the modeling job you're going to get for us."

Melanie swallowed, almost choking on the mouthful of pizza. After a brief coughing fit, she was better.

Tricia exclaimed, "Whoa, I thought we'd have to use CPR on you!"

They all laughed.

Melanie caught her breath. "From what I heard, they want all kinds of girls for back-to-school stuff. I'll ask my agent about it the next time I talk to her."

"What would we have to do?" Cara asked.

"Whatever the art director or stylist or photographer tells you to do," Melanie answered. "If he says, 'Act crazy' or 'natural' or 'scared' or 'bored,' you do it."

Jess stuck her nose way up in the air. "You mean 'bored' like that?"

The others laughed.

"Come on, Jess!" Becky said. "You can't be serious!"

"That didn't look bored," Tricia laughed. "That looked like your nose was stuck to a skyhook."

They all laughed with her.

"Then how do you look bored?" Jess asked, smiling herself.

Melanie tilted her head sideways a little and rolled her eyes skyward. "That's how I'd do it for a back-to-school picture

. . . just enough to give the idea. Not overdone like for acting so a big audience can see you. A model has to close her mind to her surroundings and pretend she's back in school, or . . . maybe on a beach, even if it's the dead of winter and she's standing on a chilly set."

"How about 'bored' like this?" Tricia asked. She tilted her head sideways and let out a discouraged breath.

"That's good," Melanie said, "except don't ever close your eyes unless the photographer says to."

The rest of them tried to copy Tricia, tilting their heads and looking just a little bored.

After "bored," they tried "happy," then "cheering for a football game." By the time Mrs. McColl brought out the chocolate nut brownies for dessert, they had tried on all of the expressions they could imagine.

"Melanie's going to get all of us a modeling job," Cara explained to Mrs. McColl.

"Oh, really?" Jess's mother asked.

"It's not for sure yet," Melanie explained quickly, feeling more and more uncertain about it.

When they'd finished the brownies and lemonade, Tricia said, "Show us how to do a modeling walk."

"You mean like a runway model for a style show?"

"Yeah," Jess said.

Melanie got up and walked over to the pool. She'd only done two runway style shows, and that was when she'd been younger, modeling mother-and-daughter clothes with Mom.

Doing a graceful turn, she tried to remember. One hand up, holding a big invisible hat from blowing, she began to glide along in a straight path toward them. About halfway, she paused and, holding up a pretend skirt slightly, smiled to one side, then glided on again. In front of them, she held up her "skirt" again and did a good turn, then headed back down the "runway" to the pool.

"Hey, that was good," Jess said, applauding. "Let me try it."

Jess's short, compact shape made her look like anything but a model as she headed for the pool. She stopped, then did a fast turn to face them, her legs ending in a tangle. Everyone roared with laughter.

"Come on, Jess!" Tricia protested, "you did that on purpose!"

"I did not," Jess answered, grinning herself. "Anyhow, let me take it from here." She began to walk toward them, trying not to grin. But her walk wasn't a smooth glide, it was more like a gymnast heading for a hard vault, and when she tried lifting a pretend skirt, she looked so awkward that they all laughed again.

"Here, let me try it," Tricia said.

Her legs had been twisted around one of the chair's wrought-iron legs, and she almost fell down, taking the chair with her, as she stood up.

"Whoa . . . graceful!" Becky laughed, and they all laughed again.

Tricia got herself together and headed for the pool. She did a dramatic turn, holding a hand to her invisible hat, but, maybe because she was still half laughing, it appeared as if she were in a crazy bank holdup. Instead of gliding, she overdid it, making it a prance. And when she arrived in front of them, she tilted her head a little and looked plain silly.

When she'd plopped down at the table again and they'd finished laughing, Jess said, "Okay, Cara, you're on next."

Cara shook her head.

"You!" Jess said. "You're not getting out of it."

Cara drew a discouraged breath and headed for the other side of the pool. She took her time doing the turn toward them, then started shyly toward them.

Melanie thought any audience would know Cara was shy, but maybe that was better than getting all tangled up. "Good," she told her encouragingly. "Don't forget the little pause for the audience at both sides."

Cara finished, still stiff in the knees.

"Okay, Becky," Tricia said. "You're next."

Becky flopped her long hair back and headed for the pool. She had nice long legs for modeling, but she was all knees and elbows when she walked. She did a quick turn by the pool and suddenly lost her balance, almost falling in.

Everyone roared with laughter again.

As Becky stiff-legged her way toward them, Melanie hoped with all of her heart that she'd never in her life have to do any runway modeling with them.

CHAPTER

7

*M*elanie was glad when "modeling practice" was over, and they all jumped into the swimming pool again. After seeing the Twelve Candles Club girls in action as models, getting them jobs with the ornery Ms. Schivitz was definitely going to be i-m-p-o-s-s-i-b-l-e.

The pool water was warm, and Melanie paddled around in the shallow end, thinking. Her new friends were so great otherwise—except for being too curious about her being Chinese—that she'd never thought of them as models. Now she saw their obstacles to a modeling career boiled down to this: Jess was too athletic; Cara, too shy; Becky, too lanky and uncoordinated; and Tricia hammed things up too much. . . .

"Come on, Melanie!" Cara said, swimming up to the shallow end. "You look too serious for a slumber party. What are you worried about?"

Actually a lot! Melanie thought. *For starters, things like baby-*

sitting . . . and getting modeling jobs for you! Instead of telling Cara, she laughed and splashed water at her. "I was just thinking about things."

"About what?" Cara asked. She stood up in the water, then made her way to one of the steps.

"For one thing, how nice it is to be here in the pool."

On the other end of the pool, Jess, Becky, and Tricia were cannonballing from the diving board into the water, but Cara sat down on the middle step. She pushed her wet dark hair back, then wiped the water from her face. "I've been thinking myself."

"About what?"

Cara glanced over at the others slamming into the pool and making huge splashes that sloshed the water all the way to the steps. "I guess you're a Christian, too."

Melanie nodded. "I've gone to church ever since I can remember . . . since I was a baby, I guess."

"I've just started," Cara said, still not looking at her. "I'm having a hard time understanding some of it."

"Like what?"

"Like how can Christians know Jesus and have Him in their hearts when He's dead?"

Melanie thought for a moment, then remembered. "My brother was just asking about that. My dad says it's because Jesus was raised from the dead. You know, from the tomb where they buried Him . . . and it's about His . . . um . . . living in us through the Holy Spirit. I don't understand it exactly myself."

"It's hard to understand," Cara said, making little splashes back and forth with the water.

"I guess it is," Melanie agreed. "In our family, my dad

knows lots about it. He says God even has a plan for each of us, but I sure don't know what His plan is for me."

"No one in our family knows the Bible," Cara said, getting up to swim. "Anyhow, thanks for explaining. I'm not sure what God's plan for me is, either. Well . . . maybe to be a writer." And, with that, she pushed off from the pool's end and began to swim toward the others.

Anyhow, it was good to know that God had a plan for everyone, Melanie reflected. Probably most people didn't even know that He did.

Strange. No one had ever asked her about religion before. In fact, no one except Dad and Uncle Gwo-Jenn talked much about it. Sure, Mom had taught them their prayers when they were little, and Silvee was learning prayers now.

Melanie suddenly remembered Bear's words: *Some Christians don't live as if they know Jesus.* . . . Maybe that meant they lied or stole or did other bad things, but she wasn't sure of that, either. Maybe it meant something else.

"Come on, Melanie!" Jess called from the deep end. "We're going to swim races."

"No way!" Melanie objected. "I'm not that good. I'll just practice by myself."

Becky won the first race, probably because she had the longest arms and legs. When they'd recovered their breath, they grinned and splashed Melanie.

"Didn't you swim in New York?" Jess asked.

"Not much," she replied, splashing them back in fun.

"You can come over and practice with me this summer."

"Hey, thanks," Melanie said. "It looks like I need to get better at it."

"Yep," Jess agreed, setting up for the race back to the deep end. "On your mark . . . get set . . . go!!!!!"

Later, they washed their hair in the outdoor shower and changed from their swimsuits into their jammies, then settled in Jess's room.

"Let's tell ghost stories," Cara suggested.

"Let's not," Tricia said. "Christians aren't supposed to fool around with spooky stuff. Gramp says—" She darted a glance at Melanie and explained, "My Gramp Bennett is a retired minister. Anyhow, he says that fear is a dangerous companion. NOT TO LET FEAR IN."

"Hmmm," Jess replied, then plopped a throw pillow on her head. "Well, why don't we do some more modeling instead?"

Not more modeling! Melanie thought as they scrambled around Jess's bedroom for things to display.

"Look," Tricia said, a lampshade on her head. "I am modeling ze very latest hat creation from Paris."

Becky pulled a pillow case over an arm, poked in fingerspace creases, and wound the rest of it tightly up beyond her elbow. She raised her arm high with great drama. "And I model for you ze latest in elegant gloves."

"Ooooooohhhhh," the others chorused. "Ooooooohhhh . . . ahhhhhhhhh. . . ."

Jess had taken a flowered bed sheet from a drawer, wrapped it around her, and stood posing on her trampoline. "And here we have the finest evening gown that money can buy. An evening gown covered with flowers and great big diamonds."

They all laughed, getting more and more wacko as they hunted wildly through her room for new ideas.

Melanie grabbed a bouquet of silk flowers from a vase and held them to a beat-up yellow backpack. Giving a low Chinese bow, then doing a graceful turn, she said, "And here, ze wonderful flowered handbag . . . very unusual . . . very expressive . . . very springtime."

When they ran out of things to model, they started knock-knock jokes, then told crazy stories about school.

"We haven't shown Melanie our klutz act," Becky said.

"No way!" Jess objected. "She's too . . . elegant!"

"I am not elegant!" Melanie told them. "I am just like anyone else."

"Okay, klutzos!" Tricia yelled. "Here it is!"

With that, they all crossed their eyes, turned their feet inward, and stumbled about wildly. "Klutz . . . klutz . . . klutz!" they chorused crazily.

Melanie started to laugh, then knew she had to join in herself. She turned her feet inward, remembered to cross her eyes, then stumbled about with them, calling out, "Klutz . . . klutz . . . klutz!"

"Oh, man!" Tricia said. "I NEVER EVER thought I'd see Miss Melanie Lin doing that!"

"I can klutz as good as anyone else!" Melanie declared, glad that dear Ms. Schivitz couldn't see her.

Still klutzing, they paraded in front of the huge mirror by the ballet barre, then fell down onto the carpet, laughing.

After they grew serious again, Becky said, "Tell us what it was like to model in New York."

Melanie sat up on the carpet, thinking. "Well, when I was in the city, I might have had an appointment to go see someone who was considering me for a booking . . . you know, a picture-taking session. There are other ways to try out for modeling jobs, but they all mean going to see the client. Models call it a go-see."

"Go see them to find out if you can get the job," Tricia put in.

"Right. A call might have come to my agency for a 'preteen size eight, fashion look, eleven or twelve years old.' That's a 'cattle call,' which means they want to see everyone in the agency who fits that description. It'd be a good chance to see my modeling friends, but I'd always look around the room to see who might get the job. There were always so many pretty girls, I'd have to remind myself that it was a question of who was right for the job."

"Then what happens?" Jess asked.

"All of a sudden, it's your turn. Front and center, facing the art director, or whoever is in charge. Gulp time. I show my portfolio of pictures in different poses. And smile-smile-smile-smile. And answer questions. Then sometimes they snap a Polaroid of you, even though they have a composite page on you in different poses. That's because models are always changing, and clients have to keep track of the latest 'you.' "

"Then what?" Jess asked.

Melanie shrugged. "Sometimes you'll get the job and sometimes you won't. A model has to think of herself as an image who's either right for the job or not. That's how to keep from getting discouraged. The other thing my dad always reminds me of is that God loves me whether I am a model or not, whether I get the job or not."

"You're right about that," Tricia said. "I heard something about having to be the right size for clothes."

Melanie nodded. "Right. You have to be a certain size at a certain age. For example, a ten-year-old should be a child's size ten. It's very hard to get preteen jobs, and it's bad for your career if you grow too fast. Another bad thing is you have to be ready to go out on a job the moment you get a call."

"Doesn't sound fair," Cara decided.

"It's a business," Melanie told them. "Just a business, and a model can't ever forget that!" The only trouble was, the more she'd told about it, the more she worried that modeling was turning into a thing of her past.

With that thought in mind, it became harder and harder to be a bright and cheery slumber-party person.

At midnight, Mrs. McColl stuck her head in the door, trying not to smile. "Now I know there's nothing you'd rather do than stay up all night, ladies, so I hate to remind you that some of you have to work tomorrow morning."

"Oh, Mom!" Jess protested.

"Oh, Mom!" the others repeated.

"Oh, ladies!" Mrs. McColl laughed. "Jess, you did promise to be a wee bit sensible," she added, then closed the door behind her with a "I'm going to trust you!"

Melanie joined the rest of them as they chorused, "Jess, did you promise?"

Jess rolled her eyes. "I did. She says if we're going to be working girls, we have to be just a wee bit sensible."

They all groaned, then finally gave in and began to settle into their sleeping bags.

"I don't like being a wee bit sensible at a slumber party," Tricia complained as the lights went out.

Becky piped in a high voice, "Don't like being sensible!"

They all laughed.

"We're not *made* to be sensible," Cara whimpered.

Finally the not-being-sensibles trailed off, and quiet filled the room.

As Melanie dozed off, she felt happier than she had been

since she'd moved to Santa Rosita. If only it weren't for the baby-sitting job coming up . . . not to mention having to get modeling jobs for these wacko klutzes!

When Melanie awakened the next morning, the phone in Jess's room was ringing.

"It's for you, Melanie," Jess mumbled sleepily.

Melanie shook her head awake. "Sorry."

She took the phone. "Hello?"

On the other end, Mom said, "Sorry to call, but Ms. Schivitz needs you to call back in an hour."

"I'll be right home!" she answered quietly and hung up.

The other girls were still sleeping as she found her white shorts and purple T-shirt and dashed to the bathroom to change. Minutes later, she was grabbing her carry-all bag, thanking Jess, and rushing out the door.

"Don't forget you're baby-sitting for the Conways tonight!" Jess whispered after her.

"I won't!"

Stepping outside, Melanie thought, *Believe me, I won't!*

At home, Mom was in the kitchen, emptying clean dishes from the dishwasher onto the white tile counter. "I hated to phone so early and take the chance of waking you girls, but Ms. Schivitz wanted to talk to you right away," Mom said. "It's strange, but I had a definite feeling that she wanted to bypass me. Her number's on the yellow stick-'em by the phone."

Melanie sat down on the stool at the tiny kitchen desk area, picked up the phone, and took a deep breath. Here was her first modeling opportunity in southern California. Whatever she did, she couldn't mess up.

She dialed the number and listened to the phone ring. The receptionist answered the phone, listened to Melanie explain, then muttered an indifferent, "Just a minute."

Finally Ms. Schivitz came on with a frazzled voice. "Melanie Lin?"

"Yes, I'm returning your—"

"Get to Price Anderson Advertising for a newspaper layout as fast as you can."

Melanie glanced down at her knee. Bicycling and swimming hadn't helped the healing one bit. "I . . . ah . . . what would I be modeling?"

"Lingerie," Ms. Schivitz said impatiently.

"I . . . ah . . . marked on my application that I wouldn't model underwear. Besides, my knee is still—"

"I thought you'd be glad for any kind of a job to get started here!" Ms. Schivitz snapped.

Melanie saw that Mom had stopped loading the dishwasher and looked worried. "I'm sorry, but my parents don't want me to model underwear. It's against our—"

Ms. Schivitz barked, "There are plenty who will!"

"I'm sorry," Melanie apologized again. Suddenly inspiration struck. "Let me tell you something, though. When I was making the agency rounds, a photographer for Wondermere Advertising mentioned they're looking for all kinds of girls for a back-to-school job, and I wanted to tell you about my four friends—"

"Wondermere? Oh, really?" the agent asked, sounding impressed.

"Yes. And the five of us are definitely a variety of girls," Melanie put in.

"I'll check it out," Ms. Schivitz replied, then hung up abruptly.

Melanie put down the phone and sighed. "She didn't even say goodbye, let alone thank me for the Wondermere modeling lead," she told her mother.

Mom's brown eyes were full of concern. "She wanted you to do underwear shots?"

Melanie nodded.

"No wonder she didn't want to talk to me!" Mom said indignantly. "If she didn't have the only agency that showed interest in you now, I'd say you should drop her. Drop her right away! What did she say about your knee?"

"I don't think she even heard me mention it. She's always in such a hurry. And now that I think about it, I don't know if she'd have told me it was underwear modeling if I hadn't asked because of my knee."

Mom shook her head. "As much as I like living in Santa Rosita, what I wouldn't give for you to still have Wilhemina de Haan as your agent!"

"That was great, all right," Melanie agreed. It looked to her now as if her career as a model was over—and just when she'd half promised her new friends, too.

"Well, you have to go on," her mother said, closing the dishwasher door. "What are you going to do today?"

Melanie got up from the telephone stool and pushed it back under the kitchen desk. "First, I have to ask Auntie Ying-Ying about borrowing her dragon head for tomorrow morning. The girls said I can be in their Morning Fun for Kids, and we're doing a Chinese dragon dance with the kids. And it's tonight I'm baby-sitting for the Conways, who live behind Jess's house on Via de Alba. Tomorrow afternoon is saved for the beach."

She didn't add that she hadn't been invited, not exactly, though it seemed like an oversight.

Mom raised her brows and smiled. "Well, it sounds as if you're on your way with the Twelve Candles Club!"

Melanie smiled a little, but didn't answer.

"Did you have a good time at Jess's slumber party?"

Melanie nodded. "We really did. They're a little wacko, but they're really lots of fun."

"Won't hurt you to be a little more wacko yourself," Mom said, grinning. "Before long, there'll be more than enough problems in life to make you too serious. Unless you turn out to be like Auntie Ying-Ying, that is. She's often very serious, but turns out to be funny despite herself. I guess you could say she's a real Chinese character."

"I guess so!" Melanie agreed. "I'm just glad you and Dad aren't such characters!"

Half an hour later, she had put her things away and hung up her bathing suit. Grabbing an apple for breakfast, she headed out the door, then through the covered courtyard for Auntie Ying-Ying's house.

"Melanieee! Melanieee!" Auntie Ying-Ying called out through the screen of her open kitchen window. "I am a very happy auntie to have you coming here. You come eat lunch with me?"

"Ah, no, I hadn't planned to. I came for just a second to ask for a favor."

Her aunt smiled broadly. "You ask auntie anything . . . anything!"

"The Twelve Candles Club girls have invited me to help on Wednesday at Morning Fun for Kids—"

She was going to explain, but her aunt said, "Tricia tell about it at you birthday party. Very good. Very much fun. What you want from auntie? You want me come help?"

"No!" Melanie objected too quickly. "I mean, we're wondering if we could borrow your parade dragon. You know, to do a dragon dance with the little kids—"

"Ah, to show Chinese culture. Very good, Melanieee! You fine culture example for us. Very good! Use dragon all you want. I have in box in garage."

"We'll take good care of it," Melanie promised. She just hoped that the Chinese bit of Morning Fun for Kids would be a success.

"I know," Auntie Ying-Ying said with pride. She smiled through the screened window. "What else new with you? Good slumber party?"

"Yes. It was a very nice slumber party."

She decided not to tell her about Ms. Schivitz and the request for modeling underwear, or her aunt would have a fit. Instead, she said, "The other big news is that I'm baby-sitting tonight."

"*You* baby-sit?!" Auntie Ying-Ying exclaimed with alarm. "You baby-sit?!"

Melanie nodded, digging the heel of her tennie in the lawn just a little.

"Who you baby-sit for? How many childrens?"

"For the Conway family. They have two children . . . a baby and a six-year-old boy."

"You baby-sit for *baby*?!" Auntie Ying-Ying asked, her eyes still wide. She was quiet for a moment, then said, "Maybe you like auntie come help?"

"No, thanks. I took a baby-sitting class at the fire department yesterday. They told us everything about it, even how to change diapers."

"Firemens put diaper on real baby?" her aunt asked with disbelief.

Melanie shook her head. "On a life-sized doll."

"Put diaper on doll?!" her aunt repeated, slapping a hand to her forehead. "Believe auntie, Melanieee. Changing diaper on real baby is no like changing diaper on dollie!"

Melanie decided not to discuss it. Her aunt hadn't even allowed Cousin Connie or her other children to baby-sit. Best to reassure her. "It was a very good class. They even taught us how to do CPR in case someone stops breathing."

"Yiiiiiiiiiiiiiiiiii!" Auntie Ying-Ying shrieked. "If baby no breathe?! If baby no breathe?!"

For an instant, fear surged through Melanie. "They said . . . it doesn't happen very often."

"One time enough!" Auntie replied. "One time plenty!"

Melanie tried to calm her aunt down, but sometimes it was impossible to reason with Auntie Ying-Ying.

Finally, when she'd calmed down a little, her aunt said, "I tell you what, Melanieee, is good thing for you and for family if auntie comes baby-sitting. Auntie has much experience with babies. I go free . . . free, no charge."

Trying to think how to refuse her politely, Melanie backed away on the lawn. "No, thanks, Auntie. But if I have trouble, would it be all right to call you?"

"Better I come," Auntie said.

Melanie shook her head. "I don't think so."

"Then I sit at telephone, wait for you call. If baby no breathe, call auntie first, then call fire department."

A wave of fear flooded through Melanie again, then she remembered Tricia's grandfather's warning—not to let fear in. The question was how to stop fear when someone like Auntie Ying-Ying brought up all kinds of awful possibilities!

CHAPTER

8

For hours, Melanie sat on the window seat in her room, reading and rereading the fire department's baby-sitting hand-outs. Birds were singing in the weeping willow tree by the Great Wall, which calmed her a lot. But she knew that if this baby-sitting job didn't go well, she'd never be invited to join the TCC, as the girls sometimes called their club.

At five o'clock, she heard Dad's car pull into the driveway, and then Auntie Ying-Ying running out to meet him. After a while, they walked over to the covered courtyard and talked, but Melanie couldn't hear their words. She guessed, though, that Auntie would try to convince Dad that she must go along baby-sitting tonight. Luckily, Mom wasn't home from running errands and grocery shopping with Silvee and William, or Auntie Ying-Ying would try to enlist them on her side, too.

Finally, Melanie glimpsed Dad returning alone to the side door of the house. After a few minutes, he came upstairs and knocked at Melanie's door. "Meli. . . ?"

"Come in, Dad," she said, stuffing the baby-sitting handouts behind the throw pillows. "I'm here."

He opened the door. "Hi, Meli," he said, beaming and spreading his arms wide for her as he came in. He was wearing a nice tan summer suit, and looked handsome and so loving.

She jumped up for a hug. "Hi, Dad!"

"Hey," he said after a moment, stepping back. "You're getting taller and taller. You're going to outgrow me."

"Come on, Dad!" she laughed.

He smiled thoughtfully, then asked, "What's that you were stuffing behind your pillows?"

"Ohhhhh!" she huffed, then had to smile, too. "Why can't I ever fool you?" She went over to the window seat and took out the handouts. "Just some stuff from the fire department class on baby-sitting."

He raised his dark brows, accepting the material from her. "I'm impressed that you girls went to a baby-sitting class."

"Auntie Ying-Ying wasn't," Melanie said, watching as he began to look through the booklets. "I saw her catch you when you came home."

He nodded, then looked through the material a few moments longer. "Hmmmm . . . this looks like very good information. I'm glad to see them giving this out."

He handed it back, smiling. "Your aunt means well, and she often brings up good points. We have to remember, though, that she's somewhat of an alarmist. It's good to be careful, but if we're always fearful, we'll never get anywhere in life. She was even worried when I first wanted to be a surgeon."

"She wasn't!" Melanie said with amazement. "Even though Uncle Gwo-Jenn was a hospital pharmacist?"

Dad gave a laugh. "She was alarmed anyhow. She'd probably have made a bigger issue of it if she hadn't also been pleased at the idea of having a doctor in the family."

"You know what she told me?" Melanie asked.

"It's hard to guess."

"That if the Conway baby stopped breathing, I should call her first, then the fire department!"

Her father looked as amazed as she felt, then smiled a little. "I've already told your aunt that I'll be on call for you, too. But I hope you know *who* to call first."

From the look on his face, she knew. "You mean God."

He nodded. "He's the one who gives us wisdom and peace in the midst of trouble."

"I don't know how to call Him," Melanie admitted. "Not exactly anyhow."

"Just pray like I do when I'm worried . . . or when I'm in trouble while operating on a patient. I say a very simple 'Help me, Jesus.' "

"I didn't know you did that," she told him.

"I say it a lot," he answered. "Before we even accept a job, I think God wants us to be well prepared. For example, I think you're well prepared to start baby-sitting. You've been with Silvee and William as babies, and you've seen them growing up. And now you've gone to a good baby-sitting class."

He smiled. "Mom told me that you turned down the underwear modeling job. That shows you're becoming more and more responsible. And, most important, that you remembered what the Bible says about your body being the temple of the Holy Spirit."

She hadn't quite remembered all of it . . . only that underwear ads were o-u-t, and that she was to respect her body.

"It wasn't . . . easy, Dad. I was worried that . . . that maybe Ms. Schivitz wouldn't ever again call me to model."

"Life's full of hard decisions," he said, patting her shoulder. "You know, Meli, when you say the Lord's Prayer, you ask for God's will to be done. It's best, though, to pray *before* you undertake anything."

Melanie let out a relieved breath. "I . . . forgot to pray about the baby-sitting job. I don't always remember."

"In this case, I've prayed for you, and God is giving me peace about your baby-sitting." Her dad smiled again, then added seriously, "I'm concerned about something else, though." His brown eyes searched hers. "I'm wondering if maybe modeling has become too important in your life."

"But being a model . . . you know . . . that's me."

He raised his brows. "You're Melanie Lin, a child of God. That's who you are, first and foremost."

She nodded, but she still felt guilty. She really wanted to keep her career going. Did that mean it was too important to her?

At ten minutes till seven, a car pulled into the driveway, and a man got out, coming to the door. Melanie was ready, with the baby-sitter handouts in her denim backpack. She remembered having been nervous sometimes when she interviewed for a modeling job, but never this nervous.

Her father opened the door. "You must be Mr. Conway," he said, then introduced himself and Melanie.

Mr. Conway was tall, dark haired, and brown eyed. He looked especially handsome when he smiled and said, "Nice to meet you, Melanie."

"Thanks. It's nice to meet you, too."

He turned to her father. "I'll have Melanie home around ten-thirty. Mrs. Conway and I are going to a meeting at the Garden Club."

"Fine," her father replied, then turning with a smile to Melanie said, "Have fun with the children."

"I will," she said, her voice a little shaky.

They left the house just in time, because behind them, William let out a loud, "Hiii-ee-yah!" Probably he'd done it to be embarrassing, but she pretended not to have noticed when Mr. Conway darted a puzzled look at her.

Out by the car, Mr. Conway opened the door for her, and she scooted into the passenger seat. It was strange to be picked up like this, she thought as she buckled her seat belt. Glancing back, she saw Auntie Ying-Ying sitting at the table in the covered courtyard, pretending to be reading the newspaper.

"That's quite an interesting wall and courtyard you have there," Mr. Conway said as he got into the driver's seat.

"Yes," she agreed.

He buckled up and started the car. "Mrs. Conway and I are on the Garden Club's Cultural Events Committee. One of our members asked your grandfather to speak to us about escaping from China and going to Taiwan."

"They've asked him to speak?" Melanie repeated with amazement.

"Yes, and he's agreed to in September for our first meeting. Your aunt, Mrs. Lin, will be accompanying him to interpret for us."

"She will?!"

"You sound quite surprised."

Melanie darted a look at him and was glad to see he was checking his rearview mirror. "I guess so. My grandfather is usually quiet." She decided not to say anything about Auntie Ying-Ying.

"He seemed very pleased to be asked," Mr. Conway said as he backed out of the driveway. "And we're pleased that he's accepted. We can read all about China and people escaping from Communism years ago, but it's never quite as real as when we hear from someone who actually did it."

"I guess not." But she thought, *If only everyone didn't treat us as curiosities! If only we could blend in like everyone else! Well, nearly everyone else!*

As they were driving out of the cul-de-sac, she glanced at Becky's and Tricia's houses. Luckily no one was out front to see her off. *If only this weren't her first baby-sitting job!*

Driving along La Crescenta, another "if only" hit: *If only she didn't have to bring over the dragon tomorrow morning for Morning Fun for Kids—and have another cultural outing!* She felt sick and tired of her family—and her—being a cultural event!

The Conways lived in a small house, the same Santa Rosita Estates model as Becky's, except it was painted pale yellow. And Mrs. Conway was tall, dark haired, and had a nice smile like her husband. Six-year-old Jason looked like them, except he was lots shorter and skinny. "I can show her stuff, Mom," he said, his brown eyes sparkling.

Mrs. Conway gave him a pat on the head. "I know you can, Jason, but since this is Melanie's first time here, it's better for me to go over everything with her."

Jason wrinkled up his nose, but he didn't reply. Melanie knew he was watching her, sizing her up.

Mrs. Conway turned to Melanie. "I already have the emergency phone numbers up on the Twelve Candles Club Baby-Sitting Sheet by our kitchen phone. There's chocolate brownies in the fridge for you and Jason," she added, leading the way to the small kitchen.

She opened the refrigerator door. "If little Pauline wakes up, here's a bottle of milk already made. You'd just have to heat it in that pot of water on the range, then test the milk on your wrist. Do you know how to do it?"

"Yes," Melanie answered uneasily. She vaguely remembered her own mother doing it for Silvee, and they'd discussed how at baby-sitting class.

"Pauline usually sleeps through the night now, so I wouldn't expect her to wake up. Why don't you come along and I'll show her to you in the nursery."

Melanie followed Mrs. Conway, whose high heels clicked along through the house. She wore a navy blue tailored dress, and seemed very efficient and organized about child care—exactly how Melanie wished she felt herself. Jason trailed behind them, and Melanie had a feeling of being watched—carefully.

"Pauline should be sleeping," Mrs. Conway said as they reached the nursery. "She's six months old, so she's not too fragile now. She's a wonderfully happy baby."

Mrs. Conway put a finger to her lips as she opened the nursery door. Inside the ruffly pink-and-white room, a white crib stood by the far wall with little Pauline asleep in it. She wore a pink sleeper and looked really funny with her bottom up in the air. Everything about her was adorable, except that she snored. Not too loud, but loud enough to call it a snore.

Tiptoeing about, Mrs. Conway pointed out the diaper-changing table, diapers, wipes, and a tube of cream.

When they left the nursery and closed the door, Mrs. Conway said, "I'm afraid that Pauline has diaper rash, so if you change her, put some of that cream on her bottom. She's such a good sleeper, though, that you probably won't have to do anything. Just peek in every half hour or so, and make sure everything's fine."

Melanie nodded. She hadn't given diapers much thought, but now that she remembered Silvee in diapers, she hoped she wouldn't have to change any. Modeling was hard work, but it wasn't d-i-s-g-u-s-t-i-n-g. Even dealing with Ms. Schivitz would be better than changing diapers.

After showing Melanie all the doors and checking to be sure they were locked, Mrs. Conway grabbed her purse from the entryway shelf. "Our other baby-sitters tell us that Jason is good about knowing what to do. Please be sure that he straightens up his room before he goes to bed. His bedtime is eight o'clock."

Jason stood beside Melanie, listening carefully.

Mr. Conway opened the front door. "Have fun, kids!"

"We will!" Jason answered.

"We will, thank you," Melanie added. She felt like jabbering, like saying almost anything to keep them from leaving, but there was nothing she could say, and then they were gone.

She'd no more than turned around when Jason said, "Now it's time for us to finish building my Lego town."

Melanie followed him to his room. "Did a cyclone hit here?" she teased, reminded of Silvee's room.

"What's a cyclone?"

"A bad wind that makes a mess of things," she explained.

He shook his head, grinning. "I did it myself."

She had to grin back. "Good job!"

"Come on," he said, "help me with the Legos."

Melanie made a space among the toys so she could sit down on the floor, then began to help him build his town. After a while, she said, "I'd better go check on Pauline now."

"Not yet," Jason said. "She just sleeps, sleeps, sleeps anyhow. She's no fun at all. I thought she'd be a sister, but she's not yet."

Melanie tried not to smile. "Okay, I'll wait awhile."

As they sat putting the Legos together, Jason asked, "Can you see like me through your eyes?"

Melanie drew an irritated breath. "You mean because my eyes are slanted?"

Jason nodded. "They're little, like you can't see much out of 'em."

"I can see plenty!" she answered huffily. Why did everyone—even little six-year-old kids—have to notice how different she was?!

"Did I ask a bad question?" Jason asked, worried.

She shook her head. "I guess not. I just wish people didn't always notice how different I look."

"You look nice," Jason told her, his brown eyes serious.

"Thanks," she said.

Later, she got up and made her way to the nursery. When she opened the door, Pauline's bottom still poked up in the air and she was still snoring softly.

Half an hour later, she went to look again, and Pauline was still snoring.

"Time for you to go to bed," she told Jason. "I'll help you clean the room." She remembered how Silvee liked racing to put things away. "Let's race to see how fast we can do it."

Luckily, Jason liked the idea, too, and the room was

straightened up in no time. Before long, he was ready for bed. His only requests were for a glass of water and to keep his door open. And he asked, "Would you give me a good-night kiss?"

Melanie grinned and kissed him on his forehead.

Maybe baby-sitting wouldn't be too bad after all, she reflected. She decided to leave the nursery door open, too, so she could hear Pauline better if she did wake up. Everything was fine, so far. Maybe she'd make it into the TCC after all.

She returned to the living room and settled down on the flowered couch with her new book, *Summer Promises*.

At eight-thirty, she tiptoed past Jason's room. Fast asleep. She tiptoed on to the nursery, and Pauline was still bottom-side up and snoring.

Just before nine o'clock, she thought she heard a noise from their hallway. Putting her book down, she hurried to look into Jason's room. He was sleeping. She tiptoed on past to the nursery and stopped in alarm.

Pauline lay on her side—and was *not* snoring.

For an instant, Melanie didn't even want to step into the nursery, then she made herself go forward. She hurried to the crib and, sure enough, Pauline seemed awfully quiet.

Melanie peered hard at her, and Pauline still didn't snore—or seem to be breathing.

Three thoughts flew to mind—phoning the fire department . . . phoning her father . . . or doing CPR before it was too late. Who knew how long Pauline hadn't been breathing?!

A numbing fear gripped her. What if she couldn't remember how to do CPR??????? What if. . . ?

Suddenly she recalled her father's words and, as she reached into the crib for Pauline, she prayed, *Help me, Jesus!* She laid Pauline on the floor, trying to remember. Tilt head back . . . next, pry open mouth—

Just as she began to open Pauline's mouth, the baby whimpered and her eyes opened wide. She was fine, after all!

Melanie almost cried with relief.

Then she remembered: The first thing to do in CPR was to make sure that the person was most definitely *not* breathing. She should have tried to rouse her *before* starting CPR!

Little Pauline stopped whimpering, focused her gaze on Melanie, and gave her a big smile. Next, she gave a happy gurgle and held her arms up to be held.

Tears filled Melanie's eyes as she hugged the baby to her chest, and Pauline put her chubby arms around Melanie's neck. "Thank you, Jesus!" Melanie prayed out loud.

Pauline made more happy baby sounds, and it seemed only a few minutes before she was asleep again.

Melanie settled her carefully in her crib. Maybe things would have gone differently if she hadn't prayed for God's help—and maybe not. She didn't even want to think about it!

When the Conways returned at ten-thirty, Pauline and Jason were sleeping, and Melanie had straightened up the kitchen, just as they'd suggested in the baby-sitting class. Not only were the Conways delighted, but when Mr. Conway paid her, he gave her a dollar tip. And Mrs. Conway said, "I hope you'll be able to sit for the children again."

To her amazement, Melanie found herself saying, "I hope so, too."

And she actually did.

CHAPTER

9

The next morning at eight-thirty, Melanie pulled Silvee's red wagon to Auntie Ying-Ying's to collect the big cardboard box with the dragon head. She'd worn a black top and slacks so her clothing wouldn't be too noticeable under the plastic dragon.

Auntie Ying-Ying already had the garage door open and was waiting. "Found old plastic dragon body, too," she said. "More better than bed-sheet dragon."

Melanie nodded. "Thanks. We'll take good care of it."

"How baby-sit go last night?" her aunt asked with interest. "I wait by phone till you come home. I wait and wait. You no call auntie!"

"It went fine," Melanie said, feeling a little guilty. "Little Pauline was as sweet as could be, and Jason even asked me for a good-night kiss."

"Smart boy," Auntie Ying-Ying joked, then turned serious.

"But everybody know babies like Oriental peoples. When we smile, *w-h-o-l-e* face *s-m-i-l-e*. Soft faces."

Melanie was unsure about babies especially liking Asians, but she did know from modeling that Asians didn't have well-defined cheek bones. And well-defined cheek bones were something most models, including her, wished for.

Well, if babies liked her face, it was good news. And Pauline had really liked her, cooing and gurgling, even though she'd awakened on the floor instead of her crib.

"Anyhow," Melanie said to her aunt, "thanks for waiting up in case I needed to call." She still felt guilty about it. When she'd been so terrified that Pauline needed CPR, she hadn't even *thought* of calling her aunt.

"I love you, Melanieee Lin," Auntie Ying-Ying reminded her. "I glad to sit by phone for many hours instead of sleep in good bed."

Melanie felt even more guilty. "I love you, too, Auntie Ying-Ying," she replied truthfully.

They grinned at each other foolishly, then loaded the boxes onto Silvee's red wagon. "You want to take big Chinese brass gong?" her aunt asked, nodding at the old brass gong that hung on the garage wall.

"No, thanks!"

"You no want to show fine ancient gong?" her aunt asked in amazement.

"No, thank you."

"How about you take Chinese sun umbrella? Parasol?"

"No, thanks," Melanie repeated.

"Maybe I come help this morning with dragon dancing?" her aunt suggested. "Good if auntie come!"

"No way!" Melanie exclaimed.

She'd no more than spoken, though, than her aunt looked disappointed again.

"I come just for dragon dance?" her aunt pleaded. "You let old auntie come just for dragon dance? Why not? Why not? What can hurt?"

"Well, since we're borrowing your dragon, I guess you can come for a minute to watch."

"Okay! Okay!" Auntie called out. "You not sorry, Melanieee! How old kids?"

"Funners. They're called Funners. And they're ages four to seven."

"Just right for plan," her aunt said.

"But you said you just wanted to watch!" Melanie protested, already sorry she'd given in. "Maybe you'd better not come after all, Auntie. It's my first time, and I'm not even a member of the—"

"I do good show!" her aunt interrupted. "I wear Chinese costume and bring paper lanterns! Oh, I think of much else!"

"It's too much trouble!" Melanie objected.

"Not for Auntie!" her aunt protested, rushing to the door leading into the house. "Chop-chop, I hurry! See you at you Morning Fun for Funners! I think of many things! I watch when kids come. Timing important, most important!"

Why-oh-why didn't I stop her? Melanie moaned to herself as her aunt disappeared into the house.

She trudged along, pulling the wagon toward the cul-de-sac, the two boxes firmly planted on it. Maybe she'd better pray about her aunt, too, she decided. *Lord, help this Chinese dragon act to go well, and Auntie not to be too wild. On top of everything else, it seems like my modeling career is almost over.*

*Please help me at least get into the Twelve Candles Club . . . and
don't let Auntie ruin it!*

At Tricia's breezeway gate, a yellow poster said,

MORNING FUN FOR KIDS
PLEASE KNOCK ON GATE

"Help!" Melanie called out. "I've got the dragon boxes to
bring in!"

Tricia opened the gate, her green eyes widening. "Whoa!
I didn't expect them to be so big." She wore a white shorts
outfit, since she wouldn't be in the dragon. "Let me open the
big garage door for you. The best way is for you guys to put
the dragon on in the garage, then when the Funners are all
here, the dragon can come running into the yard through the
breezeway."

"Good idea."

Melanie waited on the driveway until the garage door was
open, then pulled the wagon into the empty space beside Mrs.
Bennett's maroon minivan. "The boxes are big, but at least
they're not too heavy. Here, let me show you." She opened the
cardboard box with the big dragon head, which was mostly
yellow, orange, and red.

"Whoa!" Tricia exclaimed. "It's a little scary, but it's wonderful! I didn't expect it to be so colorful."

Now was the time to say Auntie Ying-Ying was coming,
Melanie decided, but Becky was just arriving, and here came
Cara and Jess down the street. They wore black tops and pants
for under the dragon, too.

After they'd admired the colorful dragon head and body,
they began to make their plans. First, they'd get the big dragon

105

head on Melanie, then Becky, Cara, and Jess would get under the lightweight plastic dragon body.

"See, there are elastic bands underneath to put under your arms," Melanie explained.

"We'll need my mother to help," Tricia decided. "She's good at costumes."

"How exactly will we surprise the kids?" Melanie asked.

"We'll get all the Funners in the yard," Tricia said, "then I'll start the magic carpet ride. When I tell the kids to close their eyes, you guys run into the garage and get into the dragon. When I tell them to open their eyes, you can come winding out through the breezeway in the dragon outfit."

"Wacko!" Jess laughed. "I've never been in a dragon."

They all laughed, and Becky added, "The Funners are going to love it."

Becky carried a small box herself. "For our crafts project, I thought we'd make construction-paper dragons." She gave a little laugh. "About the size of the 'honorable Chinese dragon' your brother gave you for your birthday."

Melanie crossed her eyes. "You mean 'lizard-sized.' "

"Probably more construction-paper size," Becky answered. "I've got lots of colorful paper."

"I'll write out today's plan," Tricia said. "Come on, help me carry the magic carpet out to the backyard."

Melanie had scarcely noticed the rolled-up brown rug against the garage wall. So this was the famous magic carpet. Jess grabbed one end of the roll of raggedy brown rug, Cara took the other, and Melanie held up the middle. Tricia pushed the button to close the big garage door, and they headed out the side door into the breezeway's sunlight.

Stepping into the backyard, Melanie was impressed. It was

a great place for Morning Fun for Kids: a colorful gym set and sandbox, a tree house in the California pepper tree, and a solid wooden fence surrounding the yard. A clay tile water fountain was perfect for thirsty kids, and the redwood table and benches were just right for crafts. The pass-through shelf from the kitchen window would help for serving snacks. Most important, there was a big lawn for the Chinese dragon to run and twist around on.

They dropped the rolled-up rug on the lawn, raising a puff of dust. "Now for the morning's plan," Tricia said, and they trooped to the redwood table. She found a pencil and began to write on a pad of yellow paper.

1) Magic carpet (Tricia starts it. Others arrive from garage under dragon.) Song: "I Am Chinese, If You Please."

2) Chinese balloon fun (Jess)

3) Dragon crafts (Becky)

4) Chinese rice pudding snack (Cara)

5) Chinese circus gymnastics (Jess)

6) Finish dragon crafts (All help Becky)

7) Free time for swings, etc. (All in charge)

"Mom's going to put on our *Flower Drum Song* record just as the Funners begin to come," Tricia said. "Now all we need is a loud Chinese gong for everything to begin!"

Don't even mention it! Melanie thought.

Just before nine o'clock, car doors slammed out front, and Funners began to arrive at the breezeway gate. The *Flower Drum Song* record started with a choppy, happy song that sounded over the outside speakers.

Becky was first at the gate, clipboard in hand, and got parents to sign in their Funners as they arrived. The Funners wore name tags on both the fronts and the backs of their shirts.

"Today we'll start with free play on the swings and in the sandbox," Becky told them. "When you're all here, we'll have a special surprise."

"Cowboy day?" a boy asked. "Another cowboy day?"

"No, something new and different," Becky told them.

Tricia's little sister, Suzanne, announced, "They didn't even tell *me!*"

And Becky's five-year-old sister whispered, "It's a secret."

The Funners' eyes opened wide, and twins wearing Jojo and Jimjim tags called out a crazy, "Umpty-dumpty-um-dum-a-lum!"

Tricia's mother was at the redwood table helping Cara start work on the dragon project. "Do you know the secret, Mrs. Bennett?" a Funner asked.

"I know something, but I can't tell," she answered, adding to the excitement.

Instead of playing on the swing set and sandbox, the Funners milled around, waiting. "Why're all of you except Tricia wearing black?" one asked.

"That's part of the secret," Jess answered.

The Funners eyed Melanie with interest, and she felt sure they'd ask about her slanty eyes.

She turned away quickly.

At ten after nine, Tricia counted Funners and everyone seemed to be there. "Okay, F-u-n-n-e-r-s!" she shouted, "let's all roll out the rug for our M-a-g-i-c C-a-r-p-e-t R-i-d-e!"

Once they had it rolled out and had sat down on it, Tricia raised her hands for attention. "Today, Funners, we're going on a magic carpet ride to faraway C-h-i-n-a!" Tricia told them. "China is w-a-y on the other side of the e-a-r-t-h! Close your eyes so we can take off!"

"Now!" Jess whispered to Melanie and Cara, and they raced to the garage. Becky and Mrs. Bennett were right behind them as they let themselves in the side door.

The moment they shut the garage door, they flew into action. Mrs. Bennett settled the shiny yellow, orange, and red dragon head on Melanie, while the others unrolled the matching plastic body. Melanie could only see through a slit in the dragon's mouth, but she'd seen enough Chinese New Year's Day parades to know what a colorful dragon looked like.

"There," Mrs. Bennett said, "you're all in. Here, Becky, hold the plastic flap to the dragon's head so you're all connected and ready to go."

"Got it," Becky said, just behind Melanie.

"Everyone ready?" Mrs. Bennett asked.

"Ready!" they all answered.

Outside, they heard Tricia and the Funners singing the "Siamese Cat Song."

Mrs. Bennett whispered, "I'll lead you through the breezeway, then head for the lawn and stay on it so you don't fall."

Let's go! Melanie thought, growing warmer and warmer inside the dragon's head.

Mrs. Bennett warned, "I'm pushing the garage door button!"

Melanie heard the garage door begin to groan upward.

Someone must have been on the driveway, because Mrs. Bennett exclaimed, "Oh! You startled me."

After some whispering and shushing, Mrs. Bennett told Melanie, "Come on . . . I'll lead the dragon's head."

Melanie moved out toward the light, seeing mostly her black slacks and shoes and the driveway. She was glad to have Mrs. Bennett leading her around toward the breezeway.

"You're all looking perfect," Mrs. Bennett told them. "Get ready to run. Now . . . now . . . run!"

Suddenly a loud BONG! filled the air. *B-O-N-G. . . ! B-O-N-G. . . ! B-O-N-G. . . !*

A Chinese gong! Melanie thought. *Auntie Ying-Ying!*

Her aunt and brother William called out "HAPPY CHINESE NEW YEAR! HAPPY CHINESE NEW YEAR!"

For an instant Melanie stopped, wishing she could die. For one thing, Chinese New Year had been months ago. For another, she had hoped fervently that her aunt—and especially William!—would not think to be part of the performance.

But Auntie Ying-Ying shouted in Chinese, then added, "Run, dragon, run! Run, dragon, run!"

Melanie ran—and just in time, too. Whoever was pounding the gong—probably William—was nearby and each hit on the gong echoed in the dragon's head. *K-A-B-O-N-G-A. . . ! K-A-B-O-N-G-A . . . ! K-A-B-O-N-G . . . !*

At first, the Funners were quiet as Melanie led the dragon in a wide circle around the backyard. Then Tricia and her mother started cheering. "Happy Chinese New Year! Happy Chinese New Year!"

In moments, the Funners joined them.

Before long, Melanie's poor head pounded with all of the loud bonging and the "Happy Chinese New Year! Happy Chinese New Year! Happy Chinese New Year!"

The noise was just tapering off when Auntie Ying-Ying yelled, "Funners, you want be in Chinese dragon?"

"Yeah! Yeah! Yeah!" they shouted. "Be in the dragon!"

Melanie saw their feet rushing past.

"Nothing to be scared!" Auntie Ying-Ying assured them. "Happy dragon! Happy dragon!"

At long last, Auntie Ying-Ying shouted, "Funners all in dragon! Run, dragon, run!"

William began to bong the gong again, and Melanie ran across the lawn. The noise echoed more and more loudly in her dragon's head, and her shoulders tired from the weight of the big head. But there was nothing to do now except to play dragon, even if it killed her.

At long last, the Funners tired, and Tricia announced, "It's t-i-m-e for our dragon to return to C-h-i-n-a! T-i-m-e for our d-r-a-g-o-n to fly! Let's get back on our m-a-g-i-c c-a-r-p-e-t r-i-d-e!"

Melanie heard Mrs. Bennett's voice amidst the loud *B-O-N-G. . . ! B-O-N-G . . . B-O-N-G. . . !* Next, she felt her nudging her along toward the breezeway.

Finally, they were on the driveway and heading into the garage. It still seemed forever until the dragon's head was lifted off.

"Whew!" Melanie said, drenched with perspiration, even her hair. "I didn't think it'd be so heavy or so echoey in there." But, worst of all, she felt like dying of embarrassment over Auntie Ying-Ying and William.

"Hurry!" Jess said. "I'm going to need help with blowing up the balloons for Chinese balloon fun."

"How are you going to make that Chinese?" Melanie asked.

They hurried out the garage door. "Who knows?" Jess answered. "In Morning Fun for Kids, things just happen!"

Indeed, things were still happening. Auntie Ying-Ying wore a red Chinese dress and carried a red parasol. She was showing Tricia and the Funners how to roll up the raggedy brown rug. And William—dressed in black, except for a stupid peaked coolie hat—was pounding the gong.

Melanie's head was still ringing when they got to Becky's dragon crafts. But Auntie Ying-Ying had a fine time telling old dragon stories while the kids cut out paper dragons. Later, for snacks, they had dried Chinese noodles that she'd brought.

"Rice pudding is not Chinese!" she told them, though she helped herself to a dish of it.

During Jess's Chinese circus gymnastics, Auntie Ying-Ying said, "Let William show ancient Chinese art of kung fu."

Before long, the Funners and Jess were chopping the air with their hands and calling out, "Hiii-ee-yah!"

Melanie caught Tricia crossing her eyes at Becky, who nodded. *After all of this, they'll never let me join the TCC*, Melanie thought. *Never!* Not only was her modeling career probably over, now she wouldn't even have friends!

The kung fu lessons were ending, and William grabbed for the big brass gong again. After ringing it three times, he yelled, "Announcement! Announcement!"

What now? Melanie thought.

"I forgot something. Melanie's agent called right after she left. She's got modeling jobs this afternoon for the whole Twelve Candles Club! You're supposed to call your mothers for permission and call Mom right back."

He pounded the gong again, as if to end the announcement.

For an instant, the entire yard was silent. Suddenly Tricia called out, "Can you believe it?! Modeling jobs! And the very afternoon we kept open for the beach!"

"Hurray!!!!" Jess, Cara, and Becky cheered.

They looked so thrilled that Melanie knew they didn't care a bit about missing their afternoon at the beach.

William hit the gong three times again, then stopped to

open a cardboard box by his feet. "Almost forgot honorable Chinese dragons!"

He opened the box, and the Funners squealed as three lizards wearing foil zigzaggy humps slithered toward them.

"Honorable Chinese dragons!" he called, then pounded the brass gong again.

This is just too much! Melanie thought as the Funners ran shrieking wildly.

Unless the girls pulled off a modeling m-i-r-a-c-l-e, her modeling career—not to mention her chances with the Twelve Candles Club—would be ruined forever! On top of it all, she must be going crazy, because she felt like yelling, "Hiii-ee-yah!"

CHAPTER

10

"All buckled up?" Mom asked. She checked the five of them from the driver's seat of the Buick and saw that they were. "Good. We're off."

Melanie sat between her mom and Jess in the front seat. Cara, Becky, and Tricia sat in back as they started out for the Santa Rosita Country Club in a strange silence.

It seemed impossible, their modeling together at a fashion show for Ames Department Store, but Ms. Schivitz really had spoken to Mom this morning. Luckily, Auntie Ying-Ying was taking care of Silvee and William, so Mom could stay to help. It was bad enough having to do runway modeling without a practice session, Melanie thought, as jittery as the others seemed. On top of everything else, a big bandage still decorated her knee.

"Tell us again about Ms. Schivitz calling," Melanie said.

Mom drove down La Crescenta. "Ms. Schivitz sounded

rather desperate. Another modeling agency had already supplied plenty of younger children and high-school models, but there'd been a goof about preteens. So Ms. Schivitz saw a big chance for her agency and offered all of you. I don't know what she told the fashion show coordinator about you, but they did say you could come a little early, since you missed yesterday's practice."

"Probably told them we're all experienced," Melanie groaned.

"Maybe not," Mom answered. "For a neighborhood back-to-school show, I doubt that modeling experience is all that important. And Ms. Schivitz seems just brash enough to grab the chance."

In the backseat, Tricia bounced with excitement. "I can't believe this is happening! I can't believe it."

Cara sounded jittery, too. "And at the country club! I've never even been there! Melanie, tell us again what we're supposed to do."

"Mom's the one to explain," Melanie answered. "She has more runway model experience than I do. You tell them, Mom."

Her mother watched traffic as she changed lanes. "The important thing for all of you to remember is that a fashion show displays clothes. It's the back-to-school clothing on parade, not you. Your movements on the runway should be natural and graceful. When the coordinator, or whoever's in charge, nods at you to go forward, smile and sweep along the runway in an easy gliding motion."

"I'd be happier if I could cartwheel down the runway," Jess grumbled from beside Melanie.

Melanie rolled her eyes, remembering when they'd "modeled" at the slumber party. What klutzes the TCC girls were—even a gymnast like Jess, who you'd think would be more graceful.

Mom laughed at Jess's cartwheeling idea, then flipped on the turn-signal for Ocean Avenue. "What's important is changing into your outfit right away. No matter how frazzled you might be while you're changing, the moment you step onto the runway, you have to look calm, cool, and collected."

As they drove along Ocean Avenue, Melanie scarcely saw her surroundings. She still felt hyper from Morning Fun for Kids and the wild dragon dance.

"How can you be calm with a big audience staring at you?" Becky asked.

Melanie knew the answer, though she was unsure if she'd remember to do it herself. "Take a deep breath and let it out slowly," she said. She'd only done two runway fashion shows in her life, but she did know about breathing. In fact, she felt so nervous now that she took a deep breath and let it out slowly for all of them.

Mom shook her head. "It's really too bad that you girls won't have much chance to practice. I'm afraid that Ms. Schivitz isn't what I'd call an ideal agent. At least she's going to be there at the style show."

"She's going to be there?" Melanie repeated unhappily.

Her mother nodded. "Ms. Schivitz is going to be there."

Melanie swallowed. "Somehow, I'd rather she weren't."

"Let's pray," Tricia said from the backseat. "That's the best thing to do."

Melanie closed her eyes and listened.

"Heavenly Father," Tricia began, "you know that only Melanie has modeling experience, and that the rest of us are new at it. Please help us to make this back-to-school fashion show a success. We don't want to let the department store or the agent down! In Jesus' name we pray. . . ." She hesitated, then added a quiet, "We love you, Jesus. Amen."

Tricia's voice had been so sweet, as if she truly knew Jesus, Melanie thought. She recalled the youth pastor's words at church: "Some Christians live as if they don't know Jesus."

Am I one of them? Melanie wondered again. *Is it possible that I've gone to church all of these years and I'm not even a Christian?* She couldn't remember ever agreeing to be one.

She did recall her dad saying, "I'm concerned that modeling has become too important to you. You're a child of God. . . ."

If only she'd told him she wasn't sure about being a child of God! If only she'd told him she wanted to be a Christian! But maybe it wasn't too late.

Her eyes still closed, Melanie prayed, *I don't know you, Jesus, and I really want to know you . . . like Tricia does. I want to be a Christian.* Tears came to her eyes, and to her amazement, she added, *I'm sorry for all of the bad things I've done. I guess I wouldn't mind so much anymore if my modeling career is over. Maybe you have something else for me to do. . . . I'm . . . I'm willing . . . to give up modeling forever, if you want me to. In . . . in Jesus' name. Amen.*

When she opened her eyes, she couldn't believe she'd prayed such a thing. She didn't want to take it back, though. In fact, she was glad she'd done it.

Slowly she felt a glow of love begin to surround her, and she knew it was from God. He loved her. . . . He truly loved her! He knew all about them going to this modeling job and how nervous she felt, and He even knew how she wished she didn't look Chinese. He seemed to be letting her know that modeling wasn't the most important thing she would ever do and that being Chinese was part of His plan for her. She wasn't merely an Asian model, but one of His children.

As if from a great distance, Mom was telling the girls how to pivot, and how to push up a collar or sleeves as they came down the runway. "And be sure to smile at the audience on both sides of you," she told them again. "Always smile."

A burst of joy filled Melanie's heart, and she couldn't help smiling like sunshine.

Santa Rosita Country Club had new red-tile-roofed buildings and a beautiful green golf course. Inside, the huge Fairview Room was lined with rows of empty chairs, and Melanie eyed the T-shaped runway with the others.

Her mother pointed at the door behind the runway, near the black grand piano. "That's where you'll come out. Let's do a run-through before people begin to arrive."

She hurried up the steps, the girls right behind her. "Line up behind me and copy what I do. Behind us is the models' waiting area, so you'll be coming from there."

They plopped their backpacks with the extra pairs of shoes in them on the floor, then stood nervously behind Mom.

"Now, we'll pretend that the last model is returning up the runway toward us. The coordinator will soon give you the nod to go forward," Mom continued. "Inhale deeply and exhale. Now, the last model is just leaving the runway, and the coordinator is nodding at you. Put on a pleasant smile and step out, gliding along smoothly. Follow me. Pretend there's an audience."

Melanie let the others go forward, then she followed behind

them. Halfway down the long end of the T-shaped runway, Mom put a hand on her hip and did a quarter turn to show off her "outfit" to the empty chairs.

"Smile at the audience," Mom said. "Be sure to smile."

"Now onward . . . gliding along smoothly."

She continued toward the top of the T and headed for its right side, where she did a graceful full turn. "Next, walk smoothly to the left side and do another full turn, like this."

As she returned up the T, she put a hand to her hip again, and halfway up the ramp, did a quarter turn for the empty chairs on the opposite side. "It's the last chance for the audience to see your outfit. Keep smiling. Think of sunshine on your back at the beach, or something else wonderful."

When they'd practiced on the runway twice, she led all of them back to the dressing room door. Inside, there were racks of clothing, dressing tables, and wall mirrors.

"Our outfits will all be on a rack marked 'Schivitz.' You each model one outfit, so it should be easy. They've given most of the work to the older models."

Other models were arriving and knew exactly where their clothes were. Even the little kids, who arrived with their mothers, acted confident.

Mom glanced through the clothes racks. "Ah, here they are. They don't care who wears what, and I've brought along safety pins to deal with size problems. We go on after the smaller children, so hurry. Each outfit has accessories in the plastic bags attached on the hangers."

Out in the Fairview Room, Melanie heard music and the sounds of an audience beginning to settle. Their murmur grew louder and louder, making the TCC girls even more nervous.

Before long, they were dressed.

Cara wore a red Tee with a denim jacket and skirt, white headband, white knee socks with tennies. . . . Jess: red sweater, plaid skirt, red bracelet, and red knee socks with loafers. . . . Tricia: green cardigan with a white blouse, green pleated skirt, white knee socks with loafers. . . . Becky: blue baggy sweater with a long pink beaded necklace and blue leggings. . . . Melanie: white sweater, purple wooden beads, purple skirt.

In the wall mirror, they looked great but s-c-a-r-e-d.

"Ten minutes, girls!" the coordinator called out. She glanced at Cara. "Oops, that skirt's too long. Pin it up."

Mom came running with a safety pin. She folded over the waist of Cara's denim skirt and pinned it into place.

The coordinator had been checking everyone. "Let's put that black pigtailed wig on you for character," she told Jess.

Jess's hazel eyes flew open and she looked as if she'd object, but she put on the wooly black wig with pigtails. She glanced in the mirror. "Me Indian squaw. Name High Leaper."

They all giggled, and the coordinator gave them a l-o-o-k, then glanced at Cara's skirt length. "Good. Now I need your names, so the narrator gets them right."

"I have it all written down for you," Mom said.

Minutes later, a woman's voice spoke over the loudspeaker, something about welcoming them to the style show. In the dressing room, the coordinator lined up the four first- and second-grade girls. "Go two by two, holding hands, and holding your lunch boxes."

The little girls grinned, walking out to the waiting area. They peered through the big one-way window at the audience without a sign of stage fright.

Melanie eyed her friends. Definitely stage fright. Worse,

she was scared herself—and then there was the stupid bandage on her knee.

"Something's wrong with my zipper," Tricia whispered.

"Let's see," Becky said, trying to help.

Melanie peered out the big one-way window at the audience and couldn't believe her eyes. Auntie Ying-Ying, Silvee, William, and Cousin Connie sat halfway up, near the runway! At least they were nicely dressed and acting well behaved.

The narrator walked to the microphone near the pianist and began to welcome the crowd to the back-to-school show on behalf of Ames Department Store. The pianist began to play again, and the narrator was saying, "We begin today's fashion show with the first- and second-grade set. And here come . . ."

The coordinator had nudged the first two little blond girls forward. They hurried along the runway, holding hands and lunch boxes, and looking adorable in plaid jumpers and white blouses.

Melanie watched as the audience *oooohhhed*, looking on appreciatively as the girls showed off their outfits.

When they returned down the runway, the audience applauded, and the next two little girls went forward in cute back-to-school pants suits.

Jess was next, and she gave her friends a phoney smile, looking even more peculiar in her black wig. When the two little girls returned, the narrator said, "And now we have the preteen set, starting with Miss Jess McColl, who is wearing a red poly-blend sweater and plaid skirt that are not only easy on the eye but easy to care for. Her red painted bracelet adds interest."

By now, Jess was halfway down the runway and had pushed

up the long sleeves on her sweater. She did her quarter turn, smiling fiercely at the audience, then continued to the top of the runway T, where she did her turns more like a gymnast than a model. But, most important, she looked good. As she returned up the runway toward them, she reached a hand up to casually show off her bracelet. Suddenly the bracelet snagged a fat black pigtail from her wig.

"Yipes!" she yelled, pulling the wig askew, and covering up one eye. She hurried off the runway, her pigtail still in the bracelet, with the audience laughing and applauding.

"Now, that is grace in spite of difficulties," the narrator remarked.

Arriving in the waiting area, Jess tore off the wig. "Just see if I ever wear that thing again!"

"And now, Miss Cara Hernandez, who is wearing that all-time favorite—denim," the narrator said.

Cara gulped and stepped out, then remembered to smile. She looked nice in her red Tee, denim jacket and skirt. Cara unbuttoned the jacket as she walked down the runway, putting one hand on her hip.

Doing a perfect quarter turn, she suddenly yelled, "Yiii!"

The audience giggled, and Cara clutched her safety-pinned side and continued up the runway. She began to take off the denim jacket, then cried out another "Yiii!"

The audience laughed harder.

By the time Cara returned up the runway, she was clutching her side and had the jacket hanging half off. She smiled desperately, making the audience applaud her all the more.

"Looks like grace in spite of a sharp safety pin," the narrator said smoothly, then paused. "And now, Miss Becky Hamilton. Becky is wearing an oversized blue sweater and coordinating leggings that look wonderful with her blue eyes. The long pink necklace adds an interesting contrast."

Becky jerked into her quarter turn, making the necklace swing wildly, but she recovered nicely. Continuing to the top of the T, she pivoted into the full turn, but her long legs caught in a tangle. She tipped, almost falling, then caught her balance.

In the second corner of the T, she pivoted into another full turn, her legs tripping her up again.

This time the audience laughed, and Becky laughed herself.

"There's nothing quite like long legs on a twelve-year-old," the narrator said.

The audience applauded, and Becky hurried back up the runway, almost tripping over her feet again.

Red-faced, she rushed into the dressing area.

"What a klutz!" she whispered to Melanie and Tricia.

Tricia grimaced. "And something still feels weird with my skirt! I think the zipper's broken."

"It can't be now!" Melanie said. "Take a deep breath!"

The narrator said, "Here we have Miss Tricia Bennett, wearing a moss green cardigan with a white cotton blouse and pleated moss green skirt. There's nothing as wonderful as green on a redhead."

Tricia glided onto the runway like a real model, unbuttoning her green cardigan, then doing her quarter turn to the audience on her right. They murmured with approval, and she moved on to the top of the T, taking off her cardigan with assurance. She did her full turn at the right side of the T, then suddenly clutched her skirt as it slipped down to her hips. At the second turn, she tried to casually drape the green cardigan over her shoulders with one hand and hold up the skirt with the other.

The audience, still chuckling over the previous girls' catas-trophes, went into hysterics.

Despite everything, Tricia returned up the runway as if she were the greatest model on earth.

The audience applauded wildly.

Suddenly Ms. Schivitz stepped into the waiting area, clutching a cup of red punch in her hand. Her sharp face filled with anger. "Are you girls trying to ruin my agency's reputa-tion?"

"We're doing our best," Melanie assured her.

"Your 'best' is dreadful! Don't you ever come looking for work with me again!"

The narrator was saying, "And now Miss Melanie Lin. . . ." and Melanie had to step forward.

Ms. Schivitz jerked away, splashing a huge blotch of red punch on the front of Melanie's white sweater.

"Ohhh!" Melanie cried out in shock.

"Your fault!" Ms. Schivitz hissed.

"Miss Melanie Lin," the narrator announced again.

Melanie stepped forward, remembering only to smile as she started down the runway. Everyone seemed to be staring at the red blotch on her sweater. Panicky, she crossed her arms over the red spot to cover it.

"Melanie Lin is wearing a white cotton sweater," the nar-rator began, making the audience laugh since most had already seen the red stain.

Melanie smiled as hard as she could, doing her quarter turn to the audience, right where Auntie Ying-Ying, Silvee, Wil-liam, and Connie sat.

"Hiii-ee-yah!" William shouted, and something crazy in her suddenly made her yell "Hiii-ee-yah!" right back. "Hiii-ee-yah!"

Everyone roared, and she continued up the runway, doing perfect full turns at each side of the T, then gliding up the runway, her arms still folded over the red stain.

The audience applauded wildly.

"A most unusual style show the preteens are presenting for us today," the narrator remarked lightly. "And now for the senior-high girls."

Melanie rushed off into the dressing room, and almost into Ms. Schivitz, who looked furious. "You girls are hopeless!" she fumed. "And that crazy yell! And a bandage on your knee! You'll never get another job through me."

"I'm sorry," Melanie said. "I'm really sorry."

"Sorry isn't enough!" Ms. Schivitz shot back.

Melanie's friends surrounded her.

"I hear Melanie's the one who gave you the lead to the show," Jess said, staring hard at Ms. Schivitz.

"And you're the one who spilled the red punch on her sweater!" Tricia added.

Mom turned to Ms. Schivitz. "I did tell you on the phone this morning that the other girls were inexperienced and that Melanie was wearing a bandage on her knee."

Ms. Schivitz backed away, heading for the door. "*If* they pay me for this fiasco, your checks will be in the mail. Don't call me, and I won't call you!" With that, she slammed the dressing room door and was gone.

Melanie glanced at Mom, who shook her head, then smiled a little as she said, "Well, you girls made the show *different*. It wasn't in the least bit dull." She gave a laugh, remembering. "I'll never forget Tricia's skirt slipping, and Becky tangling her legs—and Cara getting zapped by the pin—and Jess's wig catching in the bracelet. No matter what Ms. Schivitz says, I think it was wildly wonderful. All you girls have to get through now is the finale."

She paused. "Maybe I'd better see what I can do about Cara's pin, so she's not stabbed to death."

Tricia looked at Melanie, worried. "I hope we haven't ruined your career."

Everyone looked at Melanie, and she raised her shoulders, then dropped them and smiled. "Modeling isn't nearly as important to me lately as it once was. On the way here in the car, I told God I was willing to give it up. Now . . . it doesn't seem so desperately important."

"All right!" Tricia said.

Suddenly Melanie had to tell them exactly. "I'm really a Christian now, too."

"You're kidding!" Becky answered. "As of when?"

"In the car driving here," Melanie told them, smiling. "Right in the car, while the rest of you were gabbing."

Mom turned to her and gave her a hug. "I'm proud of you, Mel. I really am."

Melanie was too.

Seconds later, the senior-high models ran in to change into new outfits. "I don't know what's with that audience today," one said. "They want to laugh and have fun. It's not so dreadfully serious as usual."

"At least they're having a good time," another senior-high girl answered.

At last, all of the models except the senior highs were back in the dressing room. The coordinator rushed into the dressing room. "Finale time!"

She eyed Melanie and her friends, and shook her head. "You're going to have to do something really great to please that crowd now. They loved you!"

"Loved us?!" Jess repeated, yanking her black wig back on.

The coordinator nodded. "Sometimes it happens when things go crazy. But I don't see how you can top yourselves." She grabbed a big purple-and-white scarf. "Here, you can hide Ms. Schivitz's stain with this."

"Thanks," Melanie said, "and not just for the scarf." The coordinator had known *Ms. Schivitz* had done it.

The coordinator nodded, smiling, then turned to all of the models in the dressing room. "All ready now for the finale? Line up as you went out, and head up the runway in your groups."

Melanie knotted the purple-and-white scarf behind her neck, letting the fabric hang over the stained white sweater. It hid the red stain and looked rather stylish.

"All forward!" the coordinator called into the dressing room as the last senior-high girls returned.

Out in the Fairview Room, the narrator was saying, "And now for our Back-to-School Fashion Show finale! Here come our first- and second-graders, lunch boxes and all. Aren't they just darling?"

The audience applauded politely.

"And here's our lively preteens!" the narrator announced.

The audience began to laugh a little, then applaud.

Melanie beamed at them with the other girls, and suddenly the real fun began.

"Klutz-klutz-klutz!" Tricia and Jess called out. They crossed their eyes and turned their feet inward, hobbling down the runway and making the pianist play faster, crazy music.

The audience applauded more loudly, and Melanie turned

her eyes and feet inward too. Behind Cara and Becky, they all klutzed up the runway, doing awkward turns and tottering to the runway's edges, then barely regaining their balance.

The audience rang with laughter and wild applause, and William and Auntie Ying-Ying let out a few great "Hiii-ee-yahs."

"They love us!" Becky whispered from the corner of her mouth to Melanie as, side by side, they hobbled along. "They love the Twelve Candles Club . . . all five of us!"

Melanie's mouth dropped open. "All *f-i-v-e* of us?!"

Becky nodded. "Yep! We've already discussed it. You're in as a member, *if* you want to be in with such klutzes."

"You know I do! You know it!" She threw a grateful arm around Becky's shoulders and, laughing, they klutzed back up the runway together. Becky, Tricia, Cara, and Jess might never be real models, but they were real friends. It didn't matter that she was Chinese, or half Hispanic like Cara, or anything else!

The coordinator stood at the end of the runway, doubled up with laughter, and the narrator was laughing too hard to speak. In front of Melanie and Becky came the familiar call of "Klutz-klutz-klutz!" from Tricia and Jess and Cara.

"Klutz-klutz-klutz-klutz!" Becky and Melanie joined in.

The audience applauded even louder, laughing wildly with all five girls of the Twelve Candles Club.

As they klutzed along, it struck Melanie that God could take a real mess like their part in the style show and make it fun for everyone. And she smiled, knowing that He loved-loved-loved-loved them, no matter who they might be.